An Excerpt from the book

.... It was not until our visitors heard the loud *thunk* as the heavy wooden bar dropped into place sealing the door that they realized our tavern was empty except for them and us. The barring of the door seemed to encourage them since they apparently thought it meant *we* could not get away.

"And who besides you three would be here to protect us if we pay you?" Henry inquired rather politely as one of the men brought out a knife and began paring his fingernails with it.

"Three is more than enough, old man. Three is more than enough."

Saying that he was old was exactly the wrong thing to say to my new husband; that I knew for sure. He was a sensitive man, you see.

"Oh, I am sure it is," Henry said as he brought his two-edged sword up from the bench behind the table and swung it straight into the man's face with a heavy, two-handed swing.

"But what if there are only two of you?" ......

Book Nine

Castling the King

The source of the problem

The late afternoon sun coming in through the wall openings provided just enough light for the nine well-dressed and heavily bearded men sitting on the wooden benches running along both sides of the long table in the great hall of Rougemont Castle in Exeter. They had just heard someone suggest a name, and each looked at the others in total surprise to see what they thought of it.

Talking about people was something the nine of them had been doing for the past two days, as name after name had been proposed. This time—perhaps for the first time—they were all surprised. Several were so shocked their jaws dropped.

"You cannot be serious! You want *him* to be king?"

Their meeting was secret, and well it should be. All the men around the long wooden table were English barons, and every single one of them was opposed to

King John's efforts to impose common laws throughout England. They were especially offended by his law that opened the roads to everyone without requiring them to pay tolls to the barons whose lands the roads crossed.

They also did not like the King's ever-higher taxes and the scutages he required them to pay to help cover the costs of his never-ending wars to reclaim what the King considered to be his hereditary lands in Normandy and France.

The barons were desperate to restore their toll revenues and save their powers and coins. They wanted someone to replace John as King, even if it meant they had to fight a civil war to get rid of him. That their crops had just failed for the second year in a row in the midst of England's severe famine was never once discussed or even mentioned in passing.

Chapter One

The state of things.

My scarred face and slight limp shocked everyone, even though Yoram had written to alert my priestly brother Thomas about my wounds, and Thomas had quietly spread the word to the rest of my family. It surprised me to realize how much I had forgotten about being wounded until Helen gently touched the jagged scar and hugged me overly long.

"Are you trying to tell me I need my beard trimmed?" I whispered into her ear with jest in my voice and as big a smile as I could manage. Then Anne and Thomas and everyone else closed in around me, and they too pretended they did not see the long, raw scar. We all seemed to be talking at the same time as we walked up the cart path along the river to the castle.

To tell the truth, my somewhat-changed face did not bother me all that much. Now I will always look like a veteran fighting man instead of a jumped up poser with a meaningless title and some worthless lands in Cornwall that I had bought off the King with some of my prize money.

My battered face and slight limp were soon forgotten in the revelry and good will that always seems to accompany a homecoming after a successful season of sailing and campaigning in the east. Everyone was soon paying more attention to the three half-grown cats Tori had brought with her from Constantinople and eyeing the crates and coin chests the archers were carrying ashore under Harold's watchful eye.

No one asked about the crates and chests coming off Harold's galley and going into the treasure room above Restormel's great hall, but somehow everyone knew it had been another good year for the Company of Archers—and it certainly had been, despite me getting my face cut up right proper and a limp put on my right leg by someone sticking his sword so far through it that my dear, sweet Tori had to have one of my archers help her pull it out.

All my little ones and women were present when I stepped ashore, but my oldest son and heir was not. I had raised my eyes in a question to my brother Thomas. He smiled back most reassuringly and mouthed "George is fine. I will tell you about it later."

*****

Earlier in the day we had all waved and shouted our greetings as Harold's galley rowed past one of our cogs that had come in from the east. It was laden with grain and dried fish to help fight the famine threatening the lands we had bought with our prize and refugee-transporting monies. Its sail had been furled and its anchor was down; it was waiting for high tide in the light rain at the mouth of the Fowey.

When the tide came in, one of the archer Company's galleys stationed here in Fowey Village's little harbour would tow the cog up the river to the tents and hovels of our archers' training camp, where the water of the Fowey shallows just below Restormel Castle. It was the camp where the Company's archers we were starting to call Marines were being trained to fight under the direction of my land-fighting lieutenant and friend, Henry, the former crusader and galley slave from the midlands.

Henry was one of the galley slaves Thomas and I freed when we bought our first two galleys—the galleys what we bought off the poxed captain with the bezants and other coins we took off the fleeing Bishop of Damascus. That was right after Thomas killed the Bishop, and rightly so, when he tried to murder us in an effort to avoid paying the archers for fighting to defend Lord Edmund's crusader castle in Syria's Bekka Valley.

As you might imagine, the famine that has fallen on England and the food situation in Cornwall was weighted heavy on my mind when we reached our riverside camp and tied up at our little floating wharf. It was the first thing my priestly brother and I talked about after the three sisters that were my women climbed the stone stairs to talk about womanly matters in the three family rooms above the great hall where they live with our children.

My son George did not live there. He lived with his fellow students in the room next to the castle's curtain wall where my brother teaches them to scribe and do their sums and such.

"It is still bad, William, very bad," Thomas said.

"But not near as bad as it was before we began bringing in food and feeding people. Fish catches are poorly again this year, and the crops have entirely failed. There is famine everywhere in England except here in Cornwall, and we are not yet to Christmas.

"We have held off the famine here with the grain and dried fish we have been bringing in on our cogs and galleys, but things are difficult elsewhere in England.

People are reported to be starving to death and killing witches in Yorkshire and Sussex."

Then he explained my son's absence.

"George and the four older boys in the school have been a tremendous help. Whilst you were gone, I ordained them as priests and made them up to sergeants, and then sent them out to the parishes to distribute the food we have been bringing up the Fowey.

"But not to worry; some of our most dependable archers go with each of them as guards and hostlers. They are delivering the food to the parishes and making sure it is being properly distributed."

Thomas continued after a pause whilst he took a sip of ale.

"It is good experience for the boys, telling others what to do and being responsible and such. George left two days ago with some supplies for Penzance. He should be reaching there about now.

"We are using the parish churches as food distribution centers, with one or two of our more dependable archers staying in each church as acting sergeants to make sure the food is passed out fairly to everyone and all the able-bodied men and women work on the roads for what their families receive.

"At first I tried to use local people and the leaders of the hundreds to pass out the famine food, but it did not work well. Some of them tried to sell the food, and others tried to keep people they did not like from getting it for one reason or another.

"One of the bastards holding back the food was the priest at Penzance, if you can believe it," Thomas said. "Another was a Bodmin monk. He ran away when he heard what happened to the priest.

"Selling the food we were sending them, were not they and letting the people starve if they would not or could not pay. The priest even offered me a share of the coins he had been paid. I topped the bastard on the spot and pissed on his grave instead of burying him with the proper words.

"It is God's truth. I was pissing on his grave when I came up with the idea of making George and the older boys up to sergeants and using them to pass out the food."

"Aye, Thomas, I can believe it about your fellow churchmen; yes, I can," I said. "It was always been that way, has not it? So, how are things going now that you are using your students and our men instead of the local folk?"

"Actually it seems to be working out rather well, I think. Everyone that is hungry and shows up gets a full ration of bread and dried fish for the day, and the able-bodied men and women all have to work.

Mostly they are working on the roads, although, some are working on strengthening our keeps and walls and building new bridges. Quite a few families have come here for the famine food, even some of the people from the woods with the words no one can understand."

"Well, that is good news. Yes, it is. And having more men available to work raises the possibility of doing some things we have talked about before, building permanent barrack lines for the archers and their apprentices and putting up good cottages on loan lands for our lieutenants and senior sergeants.

"What do you think? Should we start building them now we have got more men off the famine?"

"Aye, we should. And do not forget, we will need some for our injured men and our widows and orphans."

******

Thomas and I and the rest of my lieutenants spent the day walking about our camp and the castle grounds, talking about many things—and especially about how George and the other boys in Thomas's school were progressing and how they might be employed in the Company in the years ahead.

Talking about the boys in his school was a discussion Thomas and I had been having for years, ever since I became the captain of the Company just before we went over the wall of Lord Edmund's castle years ago to escape the Saracens. I had led the men over the wall in the dark of night right after I gave the dear old man a soldier's mercy for his terrible wound.

Thomas informed me he now has almost thirty boys being taught to speak Latin and scribe and sum and such. He told me, with a good deal of satisfaction in his voice, that George and the four oldest boys were ordained as priests last month and are ready to permanently join the Company of Archers as three stripe sergeants, even if they look to be a mite too young for such a rank and to be priests.

Thomas ordained them? My brother has come a long way since the abbot's assistant took a fancy to him and carried him off to the monastery, where the monks taught him to scribe and sum. He bought the vacant bishopric in Cornwall off the Church with some of the bezants and other coins we took out of the Holy Land. Thomas being a bishop is important; it means he can say

a few prayers and ordain anyone he wants as a priest if
he has a mind to do it.

"It was easy to say the words to make them priests
because George and the boys in my classes were taught
how to talk and scribe Latin and pray at people, in
addition to how to push a bow and raise a pike.

"And you never can tell, can you; claiming to be a
priest and being able to say the prayers most proper
might help keep them alive if they are ever taken by real
Christians. It certainly kept me alive when the Venetians
took me. Afraid of pissing off the Church or not getting
to heaven, probably. I still do not know which it was.
Probably both."

Then we talked about something important as we
walked back to the castle for an evening meal—where
and how George and the other boys should serve when
they are finished with their schooling and go on active
duty with the Company. It was time for a decision, and it
was an easy one because we had already discussed it so
many times previously.

Each of the boys would begin his career in the
Company by serving a succession of one-year
apprenticeships as sergeants and scribes under each of
our four lieutenants and our two most important senior
sergeants, all of whom would benefit from having one of

the boys with them at all times because they can neither read nor scribe.

The Company's two most important senior sergeants—Raymond, the sergeant commanding the horse archers at Okehampton, and Randolph, the sergeant captain of our trading and money post in Rome—were among the thirteen archers that were still alive out of the original one hundred and ninety-two archers in our Company.

If we stick to our plan, all the boys being taught to sum and scribe in Thomas's school would enter the Company as sergeants and sew three stripes on their tunics as soon as Thomas decides they have been sufficiently filled with learning. They would then serve wherever the Company needs them and thereafter wherever their abilities and interests take them.

We were pleased and smiled at each other about George and the boys Thomas recruited along the way to join his school. Getting George ready to move ahead in England has been what we have been determined to do ever since he was a little tyke and came over Edmund's wall with us.

Indeed, it was all we ever talked about during those dark days when the Saracens were besieging Edmund's castle and it looked as though we would all go down.

We vowed we would spend our lives getting George and the surviving archers ahead if we escaped when we climbed over the castle wall in the dark and ran for our lives.

Chapter Two

Choosing the new king.

"He is the man you think should be the king? You cannot be serious," scoffed one of the men.

The late afternoon sun was fading and the candles being lit by the servant from the village flickered as the men sitting around the table in the great hall of Exeter's Rougemont Castle looked at each other once again. They had done so repeatedly for the past two days as name after name had been proposed.

They were meeting in secret and rightly so; all were English barons with substantial holdings, and all were opposed to King John's efforts to impose common laws and penalties and open the roads to everyone without paying tolls. They were also unhappy about the King's ever-higher taxes and the scutages he required to help pay for his endless wars to regain his family's hereditary lands in Normandy and southern France.

What united the barons was the idea that King John must go. But there was no agreement at all as to who should replace him. Each wanted to take the crown for himself, and each secretly feared one of his neighbours or enemies would get it and make his condition even worse.

"Well," said the Earl of Devon, "why not Phillip of France? We need a king, and he is got more men than all of us put together. And he certainly hates John, probably even more than we do. Best of all, he is likely to stay in Paris with his women and not object to each of us having our own laws and collecting our own tolls. We could make it a condition of supporting him."

"But Phillip's a Frenchman, a Capetian!" said a portly man at the end of the table. "We have been fighting the Capetians over Normandy ever since Edward died without an heir and William came over from Normandy and defeated Harold at Hastings. They have been our enemy since before my grandfather's time."

"They have never been my enemy, and they have never been yours; they were the enemy of the King and his family," replied the Earl. Then he added what he thought about the king's efforts.

"I do not know about you, but I do not give a rat's arse about whether the King owns Normandy or not. Do you?"

"Phillip could do it," interjected someone with the strange and distinct accent of Norman Yorkshire. "He has got enough men, and he will have more when some of the French knights come back from Constantinople now that it has fallen and the crusade has been called off."

"Well, that is a problem, is it not?" said another of the men. "Any Frenchmen that come here will do so because they do not have land in France or because they were crusaders who did not get lands of their own when they helped take Constantinople. They will expect to be rewarded with English land if they help us defeat John."

"The French knights getting some land would not be a problem," the Earl offered, "not if Phillip agreed to our fiefs and our rights in advance, including the additions from John's land and those of his supporters we would rightly claim for ourselves."

"Aye. It would not be a problem," agreed the Yorkshire lord, "but only if we get what we want and Phillip uses what is left of the King's lands to give many small fiefs to his knights as freeholds to make them petty lords. It would weaken his power to control things here in England if he had no vassals here, would it not?"

"Many small free holdings for minor French lords on the lands we do not take from John and his supporters would be acceptable to me," Devon said.

"But only if our heirs can keep our lands as freeholds without having to pay a fee to the King in order to inherit. What would weaken us all, and not be acceptable, would be if Phillip kept all of John's lands for himself or put a great lord or two over most of them."

"Aye, Devon, you are right," the Yorkshire lord agreed. "New lords that are too small to trouble us would be fine; one or two big enough to take John's place and dominate us, instead of the other way around, would not."

Then the assembled barons gathered around the rough parchment map on the wooden table and pointed and argued and told each other what lands they wanted from those of the King and the King's supporters. No one argued when the Earl of Devon said he wanted Cornwall and the north of Devon, including Okehampton.

*****

Word of the meeting of the dissident barons at Rougemont Castle and their plans for a new king did not reach us at Restormel Castle as quickly as it might have done if the roads were better.

Rougemont was at the end of the old Roman road from London that passed right under the nose of Okehampton Castle before it turned south to Rougemont and Exeter. We have held Okehampton ever since the Courtenay lord, who once held it as a freeholder, and some of his lordly friends and their retainers rode out to attack us because we were traveling on the road without paying him a toll or getting his permission.

Courtenay and his noble friends learnt something important about longbows and our new bladed pikes when they attacked us that day; namely, that in the hands of trained men longbows can be used to kill foolish lords that come out of their castles to attack travelers on the King's roads.

As a result of Lord Courtenay's attack, Okehampton now belonged to us. That was because, as the various parchments quickly prepared and registered in the parish church by my fast-thinking brother clearly showed, Courtenay sold his interest in the castle and its lands to me just before he departed.

It would look to anyone that searched the parish records that Courtenay did so just before he got himself married to Isabel of Gloucester and sold his castle and its lands so he would have enough coins in his pouch to go off crusading in the Holy Land.

We had, of course, promptly sent more than enough coins to the King for the required transfer fee. He accepted them and signed the parchment deed Thomas prepared. It granted the ownership of Okehampton and its lands to me and my heirs as a permanent freehold. That was important; it meant my heirs could inherit without having to pay any transfer fees to the king.

The contract for Okehampton was the same as the parchment contract on that John made his mark when he was Richard's regent and we bought the rights to Cornwall's manors as freeholds. That was right after we killed the old earl when he tried to take Trematon from Edmund's widow.

We used the same type of contract to get Launceston and the manors of Henry FitzCount after he slaughtered Edmund's widow and attacked us in an effort to get his poxy hands on all of Cornwall.

Courtenay did not get far on his crusade, and he never did get his hands on Cornwall or his dingle between Isabel's legs. We dumped the murdering bastard's body into a river and pissed on it.

On the other hand, we actually did help a few of his lordly friends and their supporters get to the Holy Land that survived attacking us get to the Holy Land—we chained them to the rowing benches of one of our galleys bound for Acre and sold them to the Saracens. *It was only commoners that we would not sell, and never a lord or priest that did not fully deserve it.*

Presently, as was also provided for in the parchments on which Courtenay made his mark before he departed to a better world, Okehampton is the home of Isabel of Gloucester, the woman that was once married to the King when he was landless. According to all the parchments Thomas drafted and had properly witnessed and recorded in the local parish, my priestly brother conducted the ceremony marrying Courtenay and Isabel at the same time Courtenay sold his castle and its lands to me.

That the marriage and the sale of Okehampton may have happened after Courtenay stopped breathing was not likely to become a problem. After all, no one knows for sure whose bodies were thrown in the ditch. Moreover, many witnesses made their marks on the parchment documents and, in so doing, clearly proved everything was done and recorded most proper before Courtenay sailed away to be a crusader. Who is to say otherwise, eh?

Courtenay did a good deed and probably saved Isabel's life by marrying her. Until Thomas conducted their wedding and recorded it in the Okehampton parish church, she was in real danger from the King because of their earlier betrothal that raised religious questions about the validity of his current marriage. It also was a problem because whoever married her after John died might have a claim to the throne if she was proclaimed to be his lawful wife and queen after his death.

In any event, Isabel is no longer a threat to the King. She is married to someone else, so the ambitious men of her family and the rebellious barons can never claim she is the King's widow and force her into the bed of a man they want to be king.

Isabel's situation was simple: if she ever found someone she wanted to marry, she would receive a parchment from the Holy Land sadly informing her that she had become a widow. Then she will be free to marry. Fortuitously, Thomas had already scribed the parchment with its sad message and she had it in her marriage hope chest of household items and clothes.

As it stands, Isabel's problems were all in the past thanks to the parish records that show Lord Courtenay married her before he departed to help recapture Jerusalem for the Church. As a result, Okehampton Castle was where Isabel lived and where we now based

Raymond and the company of horse archers he sergeanted.

Raymond was one of the original archers and a senior sergeant in the Company with five stripes on his Egyptian gown and his tunic. His horse archers were the men that protected the approaches to Cornwall and its roads and cart paths. The best riders among them were the outriders that spent their days riding over our lands and roads looking for outlaws and watching for potential invaders.

*****

It was a galloper from Raymond that reached us late on an autumn afternoon with news of a large party of barons and their retainers on the Roman road that ran to Okehampton and then turned south to Rougemont and Exeter.

The galloper came in immediately upon seeing them so we knew about the meeting of the barons even before it started. Unfortunately, it was more than a week after the meeting ended when an Exeter merchant told the captain of one of our galleys all about what happened at the meeting—and gave him the names of the barons that had gone with Devon to France to offer the English crown to Phillip.

We were fortunate to find out why the barons were meeting. We only found out about it because the merchant's daughter and her husband worked as servants at Rougemont Castle and mentioned it to her father when he commented he had just been down at the quay and seen the Earl and some of his men and noble friends sail off for France.

Luckily for us, and all thanks to God, one of our Company's galleys coming from London had stopped in Exeter on its way to Fowey, and the sergeant captaining the galley was smart enough to know the importance of the story he had been told by the merchant. In recognizing its importance, he marked himself as a mindful man with promise.

Was not it amazing that great lords who think they are smart enough to replace the King would think they can talk freely in front of their serfs and servants because they do not have ears and minds of their own?

Unfortunately, by the time our galley rowed up the Fowey and its sergeant captain reported the news, it was much too late to intercept the Earl of Devon and the three barons that went with him to France.

Had we received the news soon enough, we almost certainly would have dispatched all of our available galleys in an effort to intercept them and discover once again how well treacherous nobles and their men can swim.

We did not have time to do that, so I did the next best thing—I sent both a galley and galloper with parchments to King John containing the names of the barons at the meeting and those that went with the Earl to Paris to offer his throne to Phillip of France.

Another thing I did, in the hope that the three barons traveling with Devon might return from France along the same route, was to send a galloper to Raymond at Okehampton telling him to try to capture and hold any nobles or their retainers coming up the old Roman road from Exeter. I also told him to notify me immediately so I could ride over and question them, though I knew in my heart I was almost certainly closing the barn door long after the oxen had gotten out.

In any event, two days later the weather was good and I rode for Okehampton with Henry and Peter and a strong Company of archers, every man a veteran without an apprentice archer among them. Thomas and Harold rode with us, so we could talk together about how and where we would fight the French and the barons if they tried to take Okehampton or come west of the Tamar.

Harold came with us even though he did not know much about fighting on land. His expertise was that of a sailor and fighting at sea, which was exactly why I required him to come with us. He was going to have an important role in what I have in mind for fighting the French.

Harold is my lieutenant in charge of sea operations, just as Henry is my lieutenant in charge of land operations. They were galley slaves together on one of the galleys we bought off a poxed captain with the coins we took off the murdering Bishop of Damascus. My other lieutenants are Peter, my number two in the Company; Yoram, the man in charge of the Company's operations east of Gibraltar; and my priestly brother Thomas.

******

I wanted everyone to see Okehampton because it would likely play an important role if, or perhaps I should say when, we fight the Earl of Devon. Besides, I had not been to Okehampton since I "bought" the fief from the King after we killed Lord Courtenay when he and his friends attacked us on the road.

In any event, I was long overdue for a visit and it gave me a chance to ride my fine new horse—the one I took off the Algerian horse transport when we cut it out of the Algerian fleet last year. He is a beauty and there is no halfway about it. He runs faster than the wind blows, even though I am not much of a rider and have to use a saddle with stirrups and hang on for dear life.

******

Our march to Okehampton was leisurely, and we were warm enough in the fall sun so long as we kept moving and wore our cloaks and kept our hoods up. Everyone enjoyed the trip except Harold. It was the first time he had ever been on a horse and his arse got sore.

Within an hour or so of leaving Restormel Harold had switched to riding in the horse cart carrying our food and the bladed pikes and extra arrows we always carry with us whenever we travel. It brought us great merriment when he swore mighty oaths never to mount a horse again and bemoaned the fate of honest sailors who are foolish enough make their marks to join an archer Company.

"They are best for eating, not for riding," he shouted up to me with a great grimace, "and I have blisters on me arse to prove it."

We practiced with our longbows all along the way. I rode my splendid stallion and also spent a lot of time practicing the bringing of my wrist knives out from under my clothes in the blink of an eye. There were still some uneaten cattle and sheep in the fields, but the grain had failed for the second straight year.

Henry and Peter had watched me practice drawing my knives many times but never asked me about them. Perhaps it did not seem appropriate to question me, as I outranked them as their captain. For some reason, I suddenly felt called to explain how I had come to have them and how I had used them in the past. They were surprised to learn that Thomas had given the knives to me and taught me how to use them as a young lad.

It was right after Thomas came out of the monastery to rescue me from spending my life behind a plough and took me off crusading with Richard's Company of archers. He said I needed to know how to use them in case someone tried to do bad things to me. Strangely enough, I did not know how or why Thomas learnt to use them; one of the monks at the monastery taught him, I think. I asked him once, but my brother only smiled and waved away my question.

Henry and Peter knew all about my use of my hidden wrist knives at Launceston and had heard about me using them in France in front of the King and William Marshal, the commander of his army, but neither had heard the story of how Thomas and I had used them to kill the murdering Bishop that tried to avoid paying the coins the Company earned fighting for Lord Edmund.

They also had not heard the details as to how Thomas had used his knives on some of the crusaders and churchmen that tried to stop him from delivering the Pope's letter to the crusaders two years ago.

For some reason, I told my lieutenants almost everything except why Thomas taught me to use them in the first place. Thomas listened intently and barely said a word as I told the story to my fascinated men. But somehow I could sense he was pleased to have his accomplishments recognized and so obviously respected.

My lieutenants have always treated Thomas and whatever he says with a great deal of respect, even though he is a priest and now a bishop bought fair and square—as they rightly should do, since he was one of the original archers and my first lieutenant in the early days of my captaincy, long before any of them had even joined us.

We talked as we rode and then talked more as we sat around the campfire eating and drinking at night. My lieutenants' great respect for Thomas increased even more as they heard of what he had done in the early days before they joined us and of his willingness and ability to fight. I could sense it and so, I am sure, could Thomas.

By the time we reached Okehampton, we had the beginnings of a plan to fight the French and the rebellious barons if they tried to come into Cornwall.

Chapter Three

Our plans fall into place.

Okehampton was a splendid castle and quite defensible, with a crenellated curtain wall and moat around it. The October sun was still well up in the sky and warming us as we rode over the drawbridge and clattered into the castle's bailey. The archers marched in behind us carrying their longbows and long-bladed pikes and were quite impressive as they stepped together in unison to the beat of a marching drum in the cool crisp air.

Raymond and Wanda, his beautiful wife from the land beyond the great desert, were waiting with smiles and barrels of new ale for everyone. Also waiting for us was Lady Isabel with her lady's maid hovering in the background. I smiled and nodded to Isabel's maidservant, and received a curtsy and modest nod of acknowledgement in return.

I well remember being more than a little surprised and taken aback at how ever-present and watchful she was when Isabel and I first met and whilst we got to know each other.

Everyone at Okehampton took care not to stare at my face except when they thought I would not see them sneaking a look.

It was not a problem; I am getting used to it, I really am.

One of the first things we did after enjoying the welcoming food and drink, as we always do, was carefully inspect the castle with particular attention to its fortifications and siege supplies and, of course, its various gates and doors and all the ways someone might get in. The castle's readiness for a siege was more important than ever in these days of famine and rebellious barons and a possible invasion by the French. It was made even more so since we were known to be supporters of the King and the nearby Earl of Devon was the King's implacable enemy and wanted our lands.

Raymond's men were busy with their training and patrols most of the time. Even so, they had started the construction of a second wall with towers around the first to enclose a much larger outer bailey. The work had sped up recently, using the local men and women that had brought their families to Okehampton to receive distributions of the famine food in exchange for their labour.

Lady Isabel was overseeing the food distribution both at Okehampton and in the manor's two other villages. She reported there were already more than three hundred new people living outside Okehampton's walls, in addition to the servants and farmers in the castle's home village. One of them even opened an alehouse, and the village now has two smiths. There was talk, she said, about one of the new arrival's intentions to build a grain-grinding mill on the stream that brings water to the castle and its moat.

We tried the alehouse's ale that evening when we supped. It was not all that good. It was God's pity Alan Brewer is not here from Cyprus to teach the alewife how to brew good ale or show her how to add juniper berries to her brew.

Despite the availability of Raymond's horse archers, the new workers, and all the effort, the work of expanding the castle's fortifications was not going fast enough for a number of reasons—an unfortunate circumstance given the very real possibility that sooner or later we would be at war with the Earl of Devon.

In fact, the initial timber and earthen portions of the new outer wall and its towers were nowhere near complete, and the big stones that would cover them had not yet been mined from the old ruin that was on a hill about seven leagues to the north.

One reason for the slowdown was the fact that the tall trees we needed for the new wall and its towers were located some distance away. Also, we were short of the woodcutters and work horses needed to bring in the long tree trunks needed to frame the wall. Fortunately, the castle was already quite formidable without the additions still under construction.

But is it formidable enough to withstand an attack or a long siege by the French and barons, or should we withdraw to the west if they come? Launceston and Restormel are much more intimidating and defensible.

******

We gathered in Okehampton's great hall that evening to eat and drink and finalize our plans. Isabel lit three candles so we could see and had the food served and a barrel of new ale put out. Then she sent the two serving girls home to the village and she and Wanda retired to eat together in their rooms upstairs.

I had explained to the women why the servants had to be sent home—we did not want our plans leaked by the castle's servants the way Devon and the barons leaked theirs.

Raymond joined us for the eating and the long planning session that followed and rightly so, as he was one of our most experienced, five-stripe, senior sergeants and his horse archers would be in the thick of the fighting. Raymond was one of the original archers, and his men are horse archers and know how to fight on cogs and galleys as well as on horseback. It was a good thing they know both because the first fighting, so we hoped, was going to be against the French invasion fleet.

"Yes, you heard correctly," I told my men.

"We are not going to wait for Phillip's army to reach England and join up with the barons after the spring planting is finished. We are going to go after the French transports whilst they are still assembling to carry his knights and men-at-arms and mercenaries to England.

"Hopefully, we can to get to the French transports before the French troops come on board, because they will be vulnerable and easier to take or destroy if there are no fighting men aboard them to resist us.

"What we will try to do is take or destroy so many of his transports that the French King will change his mind and decide not to bring his army to England."

After a pause, I added a caution, "Phillip's deciding not to come is unlikely if he accepts the nobles' offer to recognize him, but we can always hope."

The archers and sailors we take to attack the French shipping will want to take as much as possible of it as prizes rather than destroy them. It was part of what we do for our coins, is it not? The other part, of course, is the carrying of refugees and pilgrims and money orders and cargos and such from port to port.

"Despite whatever damage we might initially do to the French fleet, the chance of conquering England with support from the English barons is probably too good of an opportunity for Phillip of France to ignore. Realistically, we are unlikely to be able to stop the French King from sending his army across the channel and trying to take England, even if our initial attack on his shipping is successful.

There are just too many French ports from which the French can sail and too many places on the English coast where King Phillip can put his men ashore and they will be welcomed by the local barons. We cannot watch them all, even if we were to deploy all our galleys.

"The most we can do is weaken Phillip's force and delay its arrival by taking a lot of prizes we can use or sell, and then doing our best to stay out of the way and keep Cornwall safe whilst the kings and the barons fight it out."

Best of all, we told each other with much drunken laughter later that evening, we will take Phillip's transports, and he will buy back the ones we do not want for ourselves so we can take them again. *We were full of ourselves as always.*

"Hopefully, if the French do come despite our attacks on their fleet, they will come ashore somewhere far away where they can do Cornwall no harm, such as in East Sussex where William of Normandy landed years ago and seized England."

What we agreed was that if Phillip did put his troops ashore in Sussex, or someplace similar, we would delay reporting when the King summoned us to join his army, and continue to delay unless the French and barons approached Cornwall, if they ever did.

We would fight ferociously if the French ever did come at us. Otherwise we would claim we were unable to help because most of our men were still away in the distant east, and those few that were in England only knew how to fight at sea, that sort of thing.

"But, by God," I announced, "we will send our galleys to take prizes from the French fleet and do all we can to prevent Phillip and his army and its supplies from ever reaching England in the first place. King John will love us for it and think we are fighting for him instead of ourselves."

"Unfortunately for us, and also for the French King, if the French come there is an excellent chance they will land their army at Exeter or Plymouth, because the Earl of Devon is not likely to oppose the landing.

"Sussex, of course, would be easier for the French to reach, but they probably will not land there because the Duke of Sussex and his men would almost certainly be with King John and fight for him."

The Duke is a relative of the King's and well known as a diehard royalist in addition to being famous at John's court for giving drinks to drunkards on the Sabbath. A famous drinker is the Duke.

"A French landing in Devon would be quite unfortunate for Phillip's pursuit of the English crown," I told my men.

"It would mean his army would have to fight our archers and pike men instead of King John's army. It would also be unfortunate for us because even the best of fighting men, such as ours, inevitably take casualties in a war no matter how superior their training and weapons. That is why we are going to avoid fighting the French on land unless we absolutely must."

I was pleased when Thomas and my other lieutenants nodded their agreement. It was important that everyone was on board with the plan, not that I would expect them to hold back even if they were not.

"In any event," I told my lieutenants, "we are going to assemble our men and weapons and be prepared to fight both the French and Devon and his fellow barons in the spring.

"What we hope most of all is that the French will mobilize a fleet from which we can take many fine prizes, and the French and the barons would fight King John's army far away from Cornwall so we can avoid being involved. It would give us a good excuse to seize the Earl of Devon's lands and Rougemont Castle with the King's blessing."

According to the merchant's daughter that overheard the barons' plans, it is the Earl's idea to merge Cornwall and Devon under one earl and the other barons agreed. My lieutenants and senior sergeants and I agree that combining Cornwall and Devon is a good idea—and that we are just the men to do it.

******

My lieutenants and senior sergeants continued to discuss the coming war at length all during our stay at Okehampton. What we decided to do was concentrate our men in Cornwall and act independently of King John without informing him or William Marshal or anyone else of our plan to attack and seize the French fleet. If the French are still able to reach England after that, we will fight them and the rebel English barons on land, but only if they are in Devon or Cornwall and only on ground of our choosing.

The decision to concentrate our forces and prepare for an all-out war on both land and sea is important. It means our men will soon be spending all their time training and getting ready to fight; they would have no time to work on strengthening our castles' walls or on our roads and bridges.

One thing is certain: we were not going to inform King John and his supporters as to how or where we intend to fight. It would be disastrous to launch an attack on the French fleet, and discover that Phillip and his men were waiting for us because a spy or one of the King's friends or women let them know we are coming.

Similarly, we are never going to fight alongside the King and his supporters on land, at least not if we can help it. One reason we will not is because we did not want to take meaningless casualties as a result of serving with incompetent leaders.

Another reason was because we did not want the King and his nobles to know how good we have become at killing knights and winning battles. Someday we may have to fight King John and his supporters. When we do, we want them to seriously underestimate us and not be prepared.

What we are also *not* going to do, I assured my lieutenants with Raymond's enthusiastic agreement, is speed up the work on our castles' defences by hauling trees out of the forest using the brood mares we have so carefully collected or the horses ridden by the horse archers. And we are definitely not going to risk any of the fast Arabians we took off the Algerians. We have plans for our horses when we have enough of them.

Similarly, no effort would be made to further strengthen Restormel and Trematon in the immediate future. It would be a waste of time since they will be virtually impossible to hold if the French or the barons surprise us by having enough strength to get past Okehampton and Launceston in force.

If the French or the rebel barons do somehow get past Launceston and over the River Tamar in force, we will likely have to take our galleys and survivors and our hoard of coins and gold and such and run for it; probably to Cyprus, I would think.

Temporarily assigning more of the men and women that come in for famine food to strengthen our key fortifications and the roads around them is the best we can do whilst we prepare for the French.

In fact, as we get closer to attacking the French fleet, there would be no one except women working in the forests and on the walls—because we would be using every available able-bodied man that is not an archer or sailor as a rower on our galleys. That would free up our archers and pike men to fight on the galley decks when we attack the French fleet.

Henry says that if Yoram gets our messages in time and the sailing weather is fair, we could have as many as twenty-six hundred archers in Cornwall by early spring plus about six hundred apprentice archers and pike men. Harold said he thinks we might have as many as forty galleys and enough extra sailors on each galley for three prize crews on each.

If Henry and Harold are right, and I think they are, it means we will have sixty to seventy archers on every galley's deck when we hit the French fleet.

Hmm. I wonder if some of the village women are strong enough to row? If they are, we might be able to attack the French fleet with more galleys.

******

I could not sleep that night. I tossed and turned and thought about things ranging from Isabel to my archers. The next morning, I set my fears aside, and scribed a long parchment describing the situation and what we planned to do about it. I sent it to Yoram in Cyprus on our fastest available galley with two non-archer rowers on every oar.

We used non-archers for the galley's rowers because we did not want to chance losing any of our valuable archers if a storm or bad piloting or pirates took it.

In my parchment I explained the situation to Yoram and ordered him to re-route all of our galleys and all available marine archers, sailors, and weapons—especially the arrow bales and bladed pikes in our

Cyprus stores—to Cornwall and to greatly increase his shipments of grain and other famine supplies.

We particularly need, I scribed, to increase the number of immediately available archers and sailors on the Fowey, and our reserves of grain and dried fish and oil so we can feed them.

Fortunately, we should have enough time to gather in what needs to be gathered and do what needs to be done to get ready for the invasion. That is because it will undoubtedly take months for Phillip to muster the French army and gather enough shipping and mercenaries together so his army can sail for England.

In four days, I decided, I would send a second and similarly crewed galley to Cyprus with the same message, on the off-chance the first parchment did not get there for some reason.

My sergeants and I think we have several advantages. For one, Phillip of France and the rebel barons did not know we are coming or how we intend to hit them.

Another advantage we have, hopefully, is Phillip's spies will not be too concerned about us because we are not knights. They know little about the Company because we did not fight in the tournaments they consider so important in weighing an enemy's fighting skills and honing their own.

In essence, my men and I believed the French and the barons will be watching the preparations of King John and his military commander, Sir William Marshal, and ignoring us.

If that is what happens, the French and the traitorous barons will not find out about our longbows and pikes until we begin killing them and taking their armour and, most importantly, the Earl of Devon's Rougemont castle and its lands.

******

Part of our plan to deal with the French and the barons is to get information as to their abilities and intentions and keep them from learning anything about ours. Our need for secrecy means only Thomas and my lieutenants can know why we are moving our galleys and men and weapons about, and how we intend to use them. Everyone else, including King John, William Marshal, and our own men, must be kept in the dark so we can surprise the French.

It also means we need to find out as much as possible about what the French and the rebel barons are capable of doing and intend to do. We need spies and we need to get them into place quickly so their information will be useful.

We should have done this years ago.

"We need more than just spies," Thomas reminded us last night. "We need their information in time for us to reach the French shipping when it is still assembling. Getting the word to us in time means we will need to have dependable couriers as well."

"Look at the map," Harold had demanded last night as he unrolled one of our parchment maps. "Phillip and his army and transports are almost certainly going to assemble near the mouth of the Seine, probably at or near the port of Honfleur.

"We have got to get someone that speaks French into one of Honfleur's waterfront taverns, with at least one fishing boat, and preferably two, standing by to carry messages. It is the only way we will ever be able to know where and when to strike."

"Yes," Henry said, "and we also need someone permanently in Exeter until it is ours and also someone on the road further to the east of Okehampton. We do, thank God, have someone in London that can keep an eye on the local barons and their shipping—Martin, if he is up to it and can stay sober."

******

Our basic plan for Exeter, Honfleur, and the road east of Okehampton was actually quite simple—spend whatever amount of coins it takes to buy an alehouse or tavern or stable and send someone who can understand the local dialect to run it. That is likely to be easier said than done, particularly since we must do it rather quickly.

My initial thought was to send Jeanette, the women that spied for us in Constantinople, to Exeter to be our local spy. Henry looked startled and nearly fell off his bench when I mentioned it.

Things must be further along between the widow and Henry than I realized, and good on them for finding each other.

We compromised—we will send Jeanette to Exeter for a week or so with one of the older archer sergeants, Robert from Rougham, and his new wife. We will also send a fishing boat with two dependable sailors who were once fisherman and are keen to be promoted. Jeanette was to return to Cornwall as soon as she got

Robert and his wife settled and properly instructed as to what to listen for and how to behave.

We will also send a rider with a horse cart, someone who can keep his horse in an Exeter stable and work at the tavern—and carry messages to us when a message needs to be carried. We will do something similar a day's journey or two past Okehampton on the old Roman road and at Honfleur using a fishing boat.

Honfleur, at the entrance to the Seine, was so important, and the winds in the channel so sudden and treacherous, that Harold decided we would need at least two fishing boats available to carry every message in case one gets lost or blown out to sea.

Doing this was also easier said than done. It meant buying the boats and finding archers or sailors that could pretend to be repairing them to explain why they were not out fishing. Perhaps they could claim to be ashore due to a leak in boat's hull that needs repairing or a fortune teller's warning.

******

Thomas decided to immediately travel to wherever King John and his court are located carrying a parchment contract for the King to sign as if we are mercenaries—but not to tell him our plans, only to get his permission to fight the French and any of the rebel barons wherever we find them.

The key provision is the contract Thomas scribed was that in exchange for the Company's services we get to permanently keep Rougemont Castle and the Earl of Devon's Exeter lands as freeholds if Devon joins the rebel barons and we can take them. Hopefully, the King will agree; he should, because our replacing the Earl of Devon would serve to weaken the barons opposed to the King.

That was our plan until one of Raymond's outriders galloped into Okehampton to report a party of a dozen or more hard-riding horsemen coming in from the east on the old Roman road. From the outrider's description of them they sounded like fighting men for sure, and there was no telling who might be coming in behind them. They could be the advance party of an invading army.

Chapter Four

We have a surprise visitor.

I ordered Raymond and his horse archers to immediately ride away from Okehampton. I wanted them to be outside the walls and available to harry our enemies in the event the approaching riders were the vanguard of a larger force. We raised the drawbridge behind them when they finished clattering out over it, and then we watched as they headed west to avoid being seen by the incoming riders.

It was probably an unnecessary precaution but good practice for a rapid movement of our forces; Henry noticed several minor problems and so did an embarrassed Raymond.

"He has not practiced them enough, has he?" Henry said to me out of the side of his mouth. We were watching an outraged Raymond shout at two laggards that were having trouble getting their weapons and supplies lashed to their supply horses.

Overall, Raymond's rapid mobilization of his men and their departure went rather well. Less than thirty minutes after the galloper entered the bailey with his message, only a handful of outriders and their horses remained in the castle along with the Company of archers that had accompanied us here.

Henry and I climbed the stone stairs at the north end of the great hall to join Harold, Peter, and Thomas at the lookout's position above the battlements on the slate roof of the keep. The highest roof of the keep was by far the best place to watch for travelers and armies on the road.

******

It was a beautiful, late October day with great white clouds in the far distance that appeared to be directly over the channel. From the top of the keep's slate roof we watched the tail end of Raymond's column of horsemen disappearing over the fields towards Launceston at a fast trot. We could also hear the sergeants in the bailey below us shouting and watched the archers of our escort Company striking their tents, carrying them into the hastily vacated stables, and moving to take up their hurriedly assigned defensive positions on the wall and in the towers. The departing archers women and children had been hurried into their stall-like homes and told to remain out of sight.

Everywhere the countryside looked normal. In the distance, we could see several ox-drawn wains moving slowly towards us on the Exeter road and a horse cart coming towards the castle gate with a huge load of hay.

"There. There they are. See them? They are on the London road," Harold said as he pointed.

"Where? Oh, yes. Can you make out how many?"

"I am not sure. About a dozen, I would say."

We watched with great and growing interest as the band of horsemen reached the turn-off to Okehampton and headed up the cart path to the castle. Perhaps it was how they rode, but somehow, as we watched them approach, we knew we were looking at a party of armed and dangerous men. There was no one in sight behind them.

There are not enough of them to threaten us. It was time to return things to an appearance of normal until we find out who they are.

"John!" I bellowed down to the senior sergeant commanding the Company of archers. "Lower the drawbridge, tell your men to hide their weapons in the stables, and get everyone back to working on the new wall."

Twenty minutes later, my lieutenants and Thomas and I were standing in the bailey as a dozen travel-worn horsemen clattered over the drawbridge and entered. They were led by Sir William Marshal, the commander of the King's army.

******

Our meeting with Sir William was warm and friendly—that somehow pleased me and made me wish to make him welcome, probably because he was a famous knight and the commander of the King's army and was not treating me as I really am, a jumped-up former commoner who was somehow able to buy a somewhat meaningless title. *But not entirely meaningless, if only because my holding it kept others from buying it and showing up to bother us.*

"Hello, Sir William. Welcome to Okehampton," I said with a smile on my face as several of the local women working in the castle hurried to the dismounting men with the traditional welcoming bowls of ale. I held out my hand.

"It was good to see you too; it is, indeed, Your Lordship," Sir William said, returning the gesture.

"And God must be with us, for you are indeed the man I have ridden to see. I expected we would have to spend many more days on the road to reach you in Cornwall."

Behind him, his men were dismounting and either eagerly grasping the offered bowls of ale or pissing. One of the knights promptly pulled down his breeches and dropped a great turd with a sigh of relief and then dipped his hand in his bowl of ale and used it to wipe his arse.

I wager Thomas is furious beneath the welcoming smile he has plastered on his face. Taking a shite inside a building or bailey is a serious offence for the men of the Company. He had read in one of the monastery's Roman scrolls that it should not be allowed, and we have always humoured him by forbidding it.

"Well then, if you have come to speak with me, it may indeed be God's Will we are met so fine," I replied. "Why not you leave your horses for my men to feed and water and come into the hall for some bread and cheese whilst you warm yourself in front of the fire."

"But first let me introduce you to my lieutenants and the Bishop of Cornwall. It is a most rare thing you have done by finding us all together. Usually we are spread out over half the world tending to our shipping and the men we have stationed in the shipping posts we have established at various ports far from England."

******

As we walked into Okehampton's great hall, I named each of my lieutenants to Sir William with a brief description of his responsibilities. Thomas I named as the Bishop of Cornwall and the man in charge of famine relief, without mentioning he was also my brother, an archer, and a key lieutenant. I explained that Thomas had come here with us to visit Lady Isabel Courtenay because she was in charge of making sure all of Okehampton's people and villages received a proper share of the relief foods we were bringing in on our transports.

I also did not mention that my brother was one of our senior commanders and an experienced fighting man, here primarily to participate in the planning for our upcoming fight with the French and the rebel barons. Sir William, in turn, named his companions as knights of his household and their squires.

Lady Isabel came down the stone stairs as we entered the hall. I motioned her forward and introduced her to Sir William, who immediately bowed and kissed her extended hand. I noticed a flicker of fear when she heard Sir William's name. She knew, as we all did, that Sir William was close to the King and does his bidding.

"Lady Isabel is the wife of Lord Courtenay who has gone crusading. She retains a residence here and enjoys our oath of protection and the right to live here under the terms of the contract we signed with her husband when we bought the place."

I said it clearly and emphatically for all to hear. I suspected Sir William knew this, but I wanted to reaffirm it for him, his men, and mine. Plus, it would reassure Isabel, should she be concerned about her safety.

Is it possible the King sent Sir William here to kill her?

"It is a pleasure to meet you, Sir William. Your honour and goodness are well known."

Good answer, Isabel; good answer, indeed.

******

Marshal was obviously as surprised to find me and my men at Okehampton as we were to see him. He mentioned it once again as we all sat down at the long table, and the castle servants and Isabel's maid rushed in with bread and cheese and more ale. Marshal and his knights sat on one side of the table, my men and I on the other. The knights' squires sat at one end of the table and listened without ever saying a word.

Sir William and his knights and my lieutenants listened intently as I explained we were here checking on the state of Okehampton's supplies and fortifications and to make sure the emergency food we were bringing in for famine relief was being distributed to all who needed it.

Later, when the food servers were out of hearing, I quietly admitted to Marshal and his men that we were still trying to decide whether or not to fight to hold Okehampton if the French or barons come this way in the spring. The alternative, I told them, was to fall back on Launceston and Restormel which were much more defensible.

Actually, Okehampton would be quite defensible with a score or two of archers and enough stores for a long siege. Marshal could see that for himself so I had no need to remind him. I mentioned Launceston and Restormel as even more defensible, even though are not, so he will think twice about coming against us.

"What we do will depend," I told Sir William, "on how many men we can bring in on our galleys before the French or barons arrive, and how ready we can get those men to fight on land. The only thing certain is we would throw everything we have into the fight if either the French or the rebel barons or anyone else, so much as sets one foot on our lands."

What I did not mention, and had quickly and quietly cautioned my lieutenants not to mention as soon as I saw it was William Marshal riding into the bailey at the head of our visitors, was our intention to attack the French invasion fleet when it was still assembling.

"Are you sure the French and barons are coming?" Marshal responded.

It soon became apparent that the King had sent Marshal to make sure I had not sent in a false alarm. I described in detail how we found out about the barons' plans, my lieutenants nodding and murmuring in agreement as I did.

Sir William listened and appeared to be convinced—perhaps because he could see the way we had people feverishly working to complete some semblance of a second wall and bailey at Okehampton.

I informed him we had already sent out the orders recalling our galleys and men from as far away as Cyprus and the Holy Land, something the King's spies would soon be able to verify for themselves. It helped when Harold nodded and glumly muttered, "All sixty-two of them," when I said we were recalling our galleys and those of our men who were willing to return.

"We expect the French to land in Sussex as the Normans did years ago, but if they land at Exeter or thereabouts, we will give them a bloody nose and hold them until you arrive with the King's army."

I told a lie when I said we expect the French to land in Sussex; we actually expect them to land in Devon. I lied because we did not want the King's army coming here and pillaging Cornwall and Devon for food and spreading their poxes, not unless and until we actually needed them—that, at the earliest, would be after we attacked the French fleet as it was being assembled.

Marshal heard Harold's comment and saw the intensity of the work underway on Okehampton's walls. I think he believed me when I said we intended to fight and fight hard. Then he asked about the castle's food reserves and the local famine situation in general; he had heard we were bringing food in from the east on our transports.

"Is it true you are feeding everyone in Cornwall?" the King's man asked.

"Yes, Sir William, we are indeed. Well, almost everyone, or so it seems. Anyone that needs food in Cornwall can work for us in some way and get food. The orphans and elderly, of course, get it free.

"We have no choice but to feed them. The grain and pilchards have totally failed for the second year in a row. Without bread and fish, the people would not be able to survive over the winter until the spring crops come in.

"I have an obligation to help them, even though I have had to go into debt to pay for the grain and dried fish certain merchants are sending us. The merchants use our galleys and transports to carry their goods, so they know they have little risk of not being paid."

We were only pretending to be poor. There was no need to let Marshal and his men or anyone else, even our own men, know we have a huge hoard of coins and gold at Restormel. If we were foolish enough to mention our treasures, the King and his knights would be more likely to come here to rob us instead of fighting the French.

Then our talk turned back to the coming war with the French and rebel nobles and our intention to fight if the French come ashore in Devon—and I repeated my statement that we would hold off the French until King John's army arrived.

"Nonsense, absolute nonsense," said a white-bearded, older knight named William Brereton sitting to Marshal's right. He ran his greasy fingers through his hair and shook his head in disdain at my statement.

"You might try to fight, I will give you that, but you would not hold the French for a minute, not one minute. You do not have a single knight or man-at-arms in your service, just some archers and sailors. Phillip's men would gallop their horses right over you."

I started to say something but bit my tongue, and motioned for Henry, who was leaning forward and about to strongly disagree, to bite his tongue.

There is nothing to be gained by letting people like Marshal and Brereton know what happens when mounted knights and men-at-arms attack archers with longbows and pike men armed with our new bladed, long handled pikes.

"Ah, well," I finally said. "You may be right, Sir William; you may be right, indeed—but we will be behind our own walls and moats, will not we? So we will whittle them down a bit, and there will be fewer of the French and rebel barons for you to finish off when you and the rest of the King's army get here."

Marshal looked at me sharply as if he had caught a whiff of irony and dismissal in my answer and did not know what it meant.

******

"I need to get back to the King as soon as possible," Sir William said. "I must let him know your warning is real. Besides, we would need to contract for certain mercenary companies from the lowlands before Phillip can sign them on to fight with the French."

I, in turn, made sure he and Brereton understood how vulnerable England and King John would be to a French invasion so long as Rougemont Castle was in the hands of the King's enemies, such as the Earl of Devon.

"Exeter and Plymouth will always be safe places for the barons to gather and the French to land until the Company of Archers holds both Okehampton and

Rougemont," I told him. "Please keep that in mind when you speak with the King."

Before he departed, Sir William and I promised to send each other any new information either of us turned up regarding the French King and the rebel barons and their intentions. Sir William specifically promised to send word when the King finalized his plan to mobilize his army and to provide us with the names of the barons that were thought to be opposed to the King.

I did not tell him we had spies in Exeter that might be able to find out about Devon's plans before he did or that we were in the process of sending spies to France to watch for the arrival and location of the French fleet that would be required to carry them to England.

Similarly, Sir William did not share any information with me about the King's spies in France or among the barons, not that I would have expected him to do so or told him about ours even if he had told me about the King's. But I do wonder if the King has any spies among the barons or, for that matter, whether he has any spies or informants in Devon or Cornwall.

We agreed to communicate by sending parchments to each other by sea via the sergeant captaining the Company's shipping post near the London wharves. We also agreed, so long as the road was safe and open, to send duplicate parchments of every message using gallopers moving on the old Roman road between wherever the King was located and Okehampton.

The King's war leader was as good as his word; he and his men mounted their horses and clattered out of Okehampton's bailey early the next day. *They must have leather arses.*

Sir William rode out over the drawbridge knowing Thomas would soon be appearing at the King's court with a parchment contract affirming our continuing and faithful support for King John, and specifying what we were to receive in return for holding Cornwall and Devon for him against his enemies—Rougemont Castle in Exeter and the lands of the traitorous Earl of Devon as freeholds.

Chapter Five

George helps with the famine relief.

Being a sergeant with my own little band of four archers to command was quite enjoyable. It was the first time I had ever really been in command of anything or been sent out on my own. The last I heard of my father, he and my uncle Thomas and their lieutenants were on their way to Okehampton for some reason. It must be important, because they all travelled together and took an entire galley company of archers with them.

I myself was in Penzance delivering two wains of famine food with John, a churl's son from Henley, as my chosen man. John was a strong archer and quite short, so he made his mark on our Company list as John Short. John and I had three one stripe archers with us, men that until recently had been apprentices.

We five were temporarily living in the priests' house of the Penzance parish church to pass out the food we brought to the local people and assign them to various work projects such as improving the local roads.

The famine was strong hereabouts, so almost everyone needed the food except the local miller. He used his wheel to grind the grain for a share of the flour.

Penzance was a problem at first. Uncle Thomas had chopped the head off the local priest when he discovered the man had been keeping the famine food away from the local people so he could sell it. That upset the local people, because they thought God's Wrath might descend on them because of the priest's death and make the famine even worse. *I myself would have been more concerned about eating than God's concern about a thieving priest.*

The people of Penzance were quite surprised when I rode in with my men and two wains loaded with food "from the good Earl of Cornwall." They were even more surprised when I showed up on Sunday as the priest in the parish church and spoke the Latin words at them and told them why they were wrong to worry about the thieving priest that got chopped by their bishop. He got what he deserved.

Do I know about such things? Of course not, but it sounded good and seemed to relieve the people of their fears. Collecting coins and saying whatever it takes to relieve people's fears is what a priest's labour is all about according to Uncle Thomas.

******

The priests' cottage next door to the little church was a nice place to live, even though it was recently departed inhabitant's head hung on a pole just outside the door and was beginning to smell most foul. Uncle Thomas had hung it there so everyone could see what would happen to someone that tried to steal the food "the good Earl was providing" or tried to avoid the required labour to earn it.

It was probably time to take it down; the birds have been at it for a while so there is not much left. He is totally unrecognizable.

A strapping woman of about thirty years by the name of Mary did our cooking and service in return for her food and a few coins each year. She did not live with us just as she had not lived with the priest; she lived nearby in a one-room cottage with her son and her mother. The three of them stood together in church on the Sunday I came to the village.

She and everyone else seemed surprised to see me when I walked in behind the cross, holding up the tattered old Bible I had found in the priests' house, and then stood in front of the little altar and began praying and chanting at them in Latin. Even the archers were impressed.

It was good fun and rather exciting. I had never prayed at people before except in practice. Next time I go somewhere, I will have to remember to bring my own Bible, the one my uncle made me copy from his when he was teaching us Latin.

Mary's husband and one of her sons had been local fisherman until their boat disappeared in a storm several years ago. Her other son, the one that came to church with her, was now working with us for his bread and dried fish. He was part of the group working to improve the cart path to the village and build a stone bridge over the little stream that runs along the edge of the village before it flows out to the sea—the one where the villagers take their cows to drink and the women draw their water.

******

"How did you learn to read and say the church words?"

Mary asked me the question most shyly as she brought me a bowl of ale when I returned to the priests' house after church. She stood next to me, and I could feel her breast rub my shoulder as she leaned over, waiting for my answer.

"My uncle taught me," I replied with a somewhat distracted smile and a catch in my throat. "He is a priest and an archer too. He is the Bishop of Cornwall even though Cornwall is so poor he does not have any priests to order about or collect coins for him. There is naught but we five new ones now that all the priests that used to be here have gone."

"I like priests. I used to comfort the priest before he was killed for his thieving. He insisted on it. He liked me to touch him and kiss him right there, that he did. Would you be liking me for that too?

"Here, I will show you so you can decide."

I held my breath. I was becoming quite certain about what was coming but I could not believe it.

"Oh my! You do like it!"

And without a further word, she knelt in front of me, pulled up my smock, and began kissing and playing with my dingle. I liked it very much and never did get to the archery tournament. One of the new archers won it.

******

"We shall all be most sorry when you are gone away and we once again have no priest," one of the smith's daughters said to me as she stood in the doorway and shyly handed me the caps she had knitted for me and my men whilst her younger sister smirked behind her.

Knitting and spinning were among the labours women are allowed to do in exchange for their famine food. The girls' mother was running errands and fetching for the men working on the new bridge; their father was the village smith.

The smith's older daughter's name was Beth. She was a tall and most comely girl. Despite her smock, I could see she had curves in all the good places just as Mary does. I could not help but greatly regretted that she was not working in the priests' house instead of Mary.

"You would like to have them, would not you?" Mary said with a warm and understanding smile a few minutes later as we watched the two girls walk away from the cottage. Then she reached for me, lifted her smock, and turned around and bent over. I forgot all about the girls.

******

Beth and Becky were both interested and curious about the strong young man, as they walked away from the priests' house. Actually, they were intensely interested in George, and it had so distracted them from everything else they had left their spinning and weaving in hopes of talking to him—and they had. It was quite exciting for both girls. Becky actually skipped for a step or two as they walked away from the priests' cottage.

"Do you think he is really a priest, him being an archer and all?"

"Maybe we should forget him, Becky," Beth said rather thoughtfully without answering the question. "He is beyond us, is not he? Besides, he acts like a priest and he knows how to scribe and sum and such. He will never do for us, no matter how much we want him."

"I know, but I cannot help it. It was all I could do not to cry when I saw him walk into church Sunday holding up the book. I thought he was an archer like the others. Do you think he is really a priest? Is it true they cannot have women?"

"It did not stop the last one, did it? Being a priest, I mean. Everyone knows he was into Mary every chance he could get and she liked it. Hmm. Maybe

Mum could find one of the fishing men or churls to wed Mary, and we could take her place. We share a bed and everything else. Why not him too?"

"Our mum would never do it," she said, shaking her head. "Da might find out and hit her."

"Then we will have to do it ourselves, eh?"

******

That evening as the sun was going down, the smith's girls walked to the beach in front of the village where the fishing men pulled their boats ashore. Penzance was a small village such that everyone knew everyone else. There were friendly greetings and smiles for the girls all along the way until they reached the man they were seeking. He was sitting in the middle of a fishing net with a great wooden needle in his hand.

"Hello, Sam. We have come to visit you with some gossip we heard," Becky the younger girl said. "It was about you and we were curious to know if it be true."

The lanky, grey-haired man sewing his net looked up in surprise as the Beth and Becky stopped in front of him.

"Hello, you two," he said with a smile. "What is that you said about gossip about me?"

"We know some gossip we are not supposed to tell you. Silly womenfolk talk about you is all it is—that someone fancies you and such."

"Who? Me? You be daft and pulling me toes; that is what you are up to."

"Oh no. I am sure it was true. She really likes you and wants to walk about with you if only you would ask."

"Who?"

"Do you not know? Why the widow Mary who works at the priest's house, of course. All alone poor Mary is these days, now that the priest has gone and her son is away all the time putting stones on the road. She is wondering why you have not been knocking on her door. Why is that?"

The next day, the girls waited until they saw George go off with his men in one of the wagons. Then they knocked on the door of the priests' house and told Mary about the gossip they had heard about Sam the fisherman wanting to walk out with her but being too shy to ask. They mentioned their willingness to take the housekeeper's position in the priests' house if she decided to take up with the fisherman permanent-like and help him with his fishing.

"Now all we can do is keep our legs crossed and pray," Beth said. Both girls giggled and pushed at each other when they realized what she had said.

Beth yawned. They were sleepy because they had kept each other up all night with their sighs and tossing and turning. Yesterday had been a busy day, and neither of them had been able to sleep last night for all their pleasurable thoughts as they tried to imagine what it would be like to have George in their bed.

******

Uncle Thomas, recently returned from Okehampton, arrived in Penzance two days later. He and four archers pulled up in front of the priests' house in a horse-drawn wagon full of sacks of famine food. George threw on his Egyptian tunic and sent Mary out the back door when he heard the dogs barking and commotion of someone arriving. He could hear people talking.

"Hello, Uncle Thomas," he shouted as he rushed out the door for a great embrace and kisses on both cheeks.

"Ah, my dear boy, how are you? How are you?"

And before he could reply, the priest inhaled a great sniff and stunned him with a question.

"And who is she, the one you have been dipping your dingle in?"

Chapter Six
A solution for the problem.

Thomas listened quietly and asked a few questions as his greatly embarrassed young nephew stuttered out his answers. As he listened, he realized the boy had become a man right under his nose. Not only was he already taller than his father, but he looked to be even stronger in the shoulders as well. It was probably as a result of pulling a bow and eating eggs and meat almost every day since he had learnt to walk and his mother weaned him.

Mary, the housekeeper, returned several hours later to set out George's evening meal. One glance and the boy's uncle was reassured; she was obviously a sturdy widow looking for a good dingle to enjoy instead of spreading her legs to trap a husband. He had not noticed her the last time he visited. He had been too busy chopping off the priest's head and helping the archers organize the feeding of the desperately hungry local people.

After he and the archers and George finished eating the suppers she prepared that evening, he followed Mary when she went outside to piss in the onion garden.

Her head jerked up in surprise, and she smoothed her skirt when he began by saying, "I know about you and my nephew."

She started to deny it but then shook her head and gave a rueful smile.

"He is a good-hearted lad. Do not be hard on him."

"I would not. Nor on you," he said whilst shaking his head. "I had not realized how much he had grown. Sometimes we forget how time flies"

Then the two of us talked about Penzance and its people and how they were coping with the famine. It soon became quite obvious Mary was a level-headed woman and knew a lot about the village. It was from talking to her that I learnt about the smith's young daughters—the two love-struck sisters that were spinning and knitting for their family's famine food—and their scheme to move in and take her place with George.

"Not that it was a bad idea about me and Sam, mind you; it was the girls. They are lovely lasses, but they are still a mite too young and may not be altogether ready to do for George until he is been learnt a thing or two more about women, and they have been learnt a lot more about men."

"Could you learn him so he knows more about women without him or anyone else ever finding out we talked and arranged it? It would be worth a lot to me and two silver coins for you; yes, it would."

"Oh, aye, I could do that; I certainly could. And it would not be much of a chore at all, would it?"

"Well then, it is settled. I will take the archers back to Restormel with me and leave him here alone for another week or two whilst you learn him a bit more. And where, pray tell, might I find these sisters?"

****** *Thomas*

The two-room, daub and wattle hovel of Harold the smith was one of the nicest and tidiest in the village. There was smoke leaking from the thatch in the roof from a fire inside and I could hear pounding and talking coming from behind it. I walked around to the back instead of to the door of the house.

A burly, grey-bearded man wearing only sandals and a dirty leather apron over his smock looked up as I came around the corner of his hovel. So did a sallow-faced man that looked like he might have the coughing pox and be about to fall on the ground. I was an unexpected visitor and they were suspicious.

"God bless all," I said with a smile as I waved my wooden cross at the two men and walked forward.

Who knows? He might be religious.

******

It took a while to convince the smith and his wife I really did want to take their daughters to Restormel to help care for my little nieces. What clinched their agreement was a gold coin for the smith, the girls' excitement when they heard they would be helping care for George's infant sisters, and an invitation for the smith and his wife to travel with me and their girls to Restormel to meet the little ones and their mothers.

I told the girl's parents they could stay there with their girls as long as they liked. The Company would always have a place for a strong and hardworking smith such as Harold Smith appeared to be.

Having William's wives teach the girls to take care of my nephew George probably was not altogether proper, so I did not mention it, even though I was prepared to sanctify it if everything worked out and the girls and George came to know each other. I also did not mention that George is my brother's son and heir or that my brother is now a newly bought noble and the captain of the Company of Archers. They would find out soon enough.

****** *Becky*

Beth and I were spinning and knitting and talking about George when our mum came home and questioned us closely about priest that prayed at everyone in church-talk before she gave us the news. We could not believe it when she explained why we would all be going to Restormel with the Bishop in a few days.

Mum's mouth dropped open when Beth and I grabbed each other's elbows and began jumping up and down and laughing and crying all at the same time. I had never been so excited in my life!

To travel as far as Restormel to help take care of George's brothers and sisters and be near him? It must be true that prayers are answered.

"Mum, does George know about all this?"

"George? Oh, the priest. I do not think so, my dear. The bishop said we would be going to Restormel as soon as George and his men return. He is apparently off somewhere delivering food—to the mine at Lannwenep, I think the Bishop said."

Chapter Seven

Freeing the miners.

My four archers and I came through the hills on the rough cart path that serves the Lannwenep mine. The last few miles were difficult because the cart path was so rough and muddy. Twice we were forced to unload some of the food sacks in order to pull one of the wains out of a ditch, and once we had to unload both of the wains to get them over a little stream.

A gaunt skeleton of a man in ragged clothes staggered up the path towards us whilst we were putting the sacks back in the wain after our second stop. His eyes were bright with madness.

"Help me! For the love of God, please help me. Something to eat. Please. Anything. Can you spare any food?" He begged in a weak, trembling voice as he stood there in his rags, shivering in the cool breeze with his hand outstretched.

John Short and I looked at each other. The man was clearly close to dying.

"There is some bread in the wain and a piece of cheese wrapped in linen on the driver's bench. Get it for him if you would, John," I said. "And cover him with one of our sleeping robes. He looks to be freezing."

Two minutes later, we all just stood and gaped as the man devoured the food, promptly retched some of it out onto the rocks next to the little stream, and then began eating again. Finally, I gently took what was left of the bread out of his hands, helped him climb into the wain, and quickly handed back the remains of the bread when he pleaded for it. He was huddled under the sleeping robe weeping and trying to kiss my hands and talk all at the same time.

His story chilled my heart and caused me to adjust the wrist knives Uncle Thomas insisted I always wear hidden under my tunic and pull my sword. As I did I told tell my men to arm themselves and string their bows.

******

We followed the path along the stream as it ran around a tree-covered little hill. We moved slowly towards a chimneyless cottage with a thatched roof and three long, barnlike hovels.

The slave barns were probably where the starving slave and his fellow slaves had lived before the overseers stopped feeding them and left them to die. The walls and other remnants of a stone building stood next to the little stream. It looked like it had not been used for many years. There was obviously a fire inside the cottage, as we could see wisps of wood smoke coming out of the thatch in several places at the south end.

Suddenly, two haggard shivering men appeared out of nowhere. They were dressed in rags and called out in pitiful voices as they began staggering up the path towards us with their arms outstretched and pleading. A few moments later, a man that walked and looked as if he might be strong and able-bodied came out of the cottage next to the slave barns in response to all the commotion.

The man that came to the cottage door took one look at us and our wains and hurried back inside. Seconds later, three men came out carrying whips and clubs. One of them scurried towards the entrance of a tunnel cut into the nearby hill; the other two just stood there and watched us as we clattered down the rough path to where they were standing.

We had obviously reached the King's mine and the building where the first refining of tin is done. It was rundown and obviously no longer in use.

The old building had probably been used before the firewood hereabouts ran out and the refinery at Truro opened. There are big trees all about, so this must be quite an old mine; maybe it was even one of the Roman mines Uncle Thomas told us about.

By the time our wains reached the waiting men, two more men came out of the entrance of the tunnel and headed towards us, along with the man that had obviously been sent to fetch them. So did two ragged men that came out of one of the slave barns.

"What are you doing here?" one of the men demanded with his hands on his hips, as our two wains rolled to a stop in front of the cottage.

Our questioner was a bulky fellow with a greasy, red beard. He was wearing a filthy, hooded, sheepskin cloak over his shirt, and he carried a whip and a heavy club. Despite the chill in the air, his hood was down so he could see and hear.

I did not immediately respond. Instead, I smiled and raised my hand in greeting as John and I jumped down. The archers driving our two wains reined in their horses and climbed down to hobble them.

"I asked you what you are doing here," the bulky man repeated, this time with a snarling threat of real menace in his voice.

"We have brought famine food from the Earl of Cornwall on whose lands you are standing. Who are you?"

"I am captain of the King's mine and his slaves, boy, that is who I am. So you leave your food with me and get yourselves gone before I put you in chains and work you for the King."

Boy am I? I will show you boy, you insulting sonofabitch.

"That is the mine over there, and it is indeed the King's," I said as I pointed at the tunnel entrance. And then I pointed to where he was standing and put him in his place.

"And that land you are standing on is the Earl's land, so mind your tongue. Now, what is this about slaves, and why are these men starving?"

"Them slaves be my business, not yours. Now, you be a good little lad and unload your wains as you are supposed to do and get you gone." He walked up to me and poked me hard in the chest with the handle of his whip as he ordered me to go. He held his club as if ready to swing it.

Perhaps what happened next was instinct. Perhaps it was my need to save face in front of my men. I did not know what it was. My blood was boiling.

My wrist knives slipped out of their sheaths and down into my hands. In the blink of an eye, as the butt of his whip hit my chest, I jammed them as far as they would go into both sides of the slaver's neck. He did not even have time to flinch or swing his club before I took him.

He stared at me in surprise and disbelief as I gave both knives a good pull and finished him off just as Uncle Thomas had taught me. And then, for some reason, I held him up by the knives' handles and stared back at him for several seconds. We stood there nose to nose as great gushes of blood spouted out of his neck. He was the first man I had ever killed; it was easier than I expected.

The slaver's men surged forward and raised their clubs as soon as the big man and I came together. John Short was much faster than they were, and he had pulled his sword as soon as he saw the man approach me with a whip and a club and an unfriendly look on his face. The closest man was still raising his club when John's sword damn near took off his head. He did not even have time to scream.

The other slavers stopped with stunned looks on their faces. Then they turned around and ran as John's man slumped to the ground. I finally jerked my knives out of the dead slaver and let him fall as well.

As he fell, I heard the familiar *thud* as an arrow hit its target and looked up to watch as the most distant of the running men went down on one knee and began a high-pitched scream. One of the new archers had jumped down from the wain when John and I went into action. His name was Edward and he was obviously a fast thinker and good shot.

I waved my hand just in time to stop him from launching a second arrow to take another of the overseers. *And later I was sorry I did; the bastard got clean away.*

"Let them go," I shouted. A few seconds later, the screaming trailed away to a whimper and the slaver holding on to the arrow sticking out of his belly with both hands fell over on his side.

I am trembling for some reason. I wonder why?

We quickly finished hobbling the horses. Then all five of us nocked arrows in our bows and I led the way as we moved to cautiously investigate buildings around the mine entrance. First we looked into the slavers' smoke-filled cottage. It turned out to be empty except for three slatternly women that apparently belonged to the slavers. Then we walked to the tunnel entrance where the surviving whip carriers had run.

That is *a damn foolish thing for them to do unless there is another way to get out.*

The raggedy and shivering men just stood there the entire time gaping at us in disbelief without saying a word. One of them had his hand out as if to speak the entire time.

"Come out. We would not kill you. We have brought food from the Earl of Cornwall."

I shouted my message into the tunnel entrance, first in Norman French and then in the dialect we use in camp and in our family, the one some now call English. After a few moments, there was some kind of answer from inside. I could not understand it. There was some sort of light flickering a good distance into the tunnel.

My men shook their heads when I looked at them. They could not understand what had been said either. I moved two or three feet closer and shouted out my message once again as loud as I could.

After a brief wait there was a rustle and clanking from in the tunnel, and a half-naked scarecrow carrying a candle lantern emerged into the daylight. We watched as at least forty filthy, ragged men walked slowly out of the tunnel. The left leg of every one of them was attached to a long chain. Two of the men were carrying wooden shovels, but on the backs of all the others were woven baskets full of rocks. Not one of the whip carriers came out with them.

"Do any of you speak English? Is anyone else in the mine?" I shouted as they came out. "Is anyone else in the mine?"

A man near the end of the chain finally answered in heavily accented English.

"There are two other chains like this one in the mine. They do the digging and clear the fall. We are the carriers. Who are you?"

None of the other slaves answered me or even attempted to speak. My first thought was that they must be foreigners and cannot understand me.

I ignored the slave's question and asked my own as my men gathered around me and stared in disbelief at the shivering, chained men that were blinking and shielding their eyes from the sudden light of the sun.

"What happened to the men with whips, the ones that just ran into the mine? Who has the key to unlock the chain?"

I asked my questions as I approached them. The man that had spoken out just stood there and looked at me with a great deal of fear and worry in his eyes. The others would not look at me; they averted their eyes and stared at their feet.

"They ran past us and into the upper shaft," the man finally said in broken English. He started to continue but suddenly stopped as if he had made a terrible mistake in talking to me. But then he rallied and continued.

"Captain Sam is the one what has the key. He is mostly over there where he and the other drivers live," he said as he pointed to the cottage from which one of the men we killed had come.

The three ragged women we found in the slavers' cottage came out whilst we were standing next to the chain of men. They just stood there unmoving and looked at us. Suddenly, one of them screamed and pointed, and they all ran to where the men we had killed lay crumpled on the ground—and began hysterically picking up big rocks and smashing them down on the head of one of the dead men.

"John," I said to my chosen man, "I think we just found the mine captain. Better run over there and see if you can find the key before the women destroy it."

******

It took all that day and much of the next to sort things out. I began by ordering the archers to bring some of the sacks of dried little fishes down from the wains and give each of the chained men six of them to eat and some to the scarecrows as well. The fish came from somewhere in the east and were slightly larger than the pilchards that were often dried and eaten in these parts.

Whilst John was off to search for the key, the line of chained men put down their wicker baskets and shuffled their way to the little stream that ran through the mine camp. Not a word was spoken. The way they did it made me think it was part of their daily routine.

It was whilst the men were kneeling along the stream drinking water from it that we began unlocking their ankle chains and giving them their fish. The men never said a word even though they appeared to be incredibly grateful and ate ravenously.

The slaves ate and watched silently as John and one of the new archers moved down the chain using the key to free them. They just stood there with shocked looks on their faces even after they were freed.

It was not until later we would learn that they had been beaten and starved by the slavers if they spoke so much as a single word.

Whilst the chained men were being unlocked, two more scarecrows staggered out of the three rough, barnlike hovels where the slaves apparently were quartered when not at their labours. They tried to make their way to us making pitiful cries and holding out their hands as beggars. One of them went down on his knees and fell to the ground. He was struggling to get up so I picked up a handful of fish from one of the bales and walked over to give them to the poor sod and help him to his feet. That is when I found the full horror of the place.

I was handing a dried fish to the man on the ground when I looked past him and into the entrance of the barnlike hovel. There was a body on the dirt floor just inside the door.

"John!" I shouted over my shoulder as I started for the entrance. "You stay there and mind the food and wains. The rest of you get over here and look alert. Swords and bows ready. Check out the barns; see if anyone is in them."

******

What we found and learnt was horrible. There were dead and dying men in every slave barn. Apparently, those that became so weak they could no longer be made to work were unchained and left to starve to death.

I took one look inside the slave barn and shouted to the man that spoke English. I told him to order the men that had already been released from the long chain to come help us.

"And you come here and help too," I called out to the three women. They had climbed up onto one of our wains and were busy stuffing themselves with dried fish from one of the sacks that had broken open.

We carried the starving men out into the sunlight and tried to save them. We used the water skin we had brought with us and some of the wooden food bowls we found in the slave barns to bring them water whilst we covered them with some of the filthy bedding John found in one of the slave barns and tried to feed them. The dead we left in the slave barns where they lay.

The slaves were docile and did whatever we told them to do without a word of disagreement or protest. Almost immediately I assigned three of them to bring water and fish to the seven men we found in the barns that were alive but too weak to stand.

More and more of the slaves began to speak as they ate—in English. Suddenly, it was as if a weir had broken, and their words came out in a great torrent. They were, to hear them tell it, mostly serfs and churls and even franklins that had been picked up by wandering bands of slave takers. They had been brought to the mine in chains and told by the captain of the slave drivers, the man I had killed, and now belonged to the King.

English slaves belonging to a king who claims to follow the Church, that forbids Christians from owning slaves unless they are heretics? Is that possible? I know the Church has serfs who cannot leave its lands, but I thought the Church was opposed to slaves unless it owned them. Well, they were free now, so the blame is mine if the King gets angry; I hope Uncle Thomas was right when he told us the King is far away and neither knows nor cares about folk such as these.

******

Darkness fell and things became even more hectic as another long chain of men came out of the mine, followed shortly by another. The missing overseers still did not appear.

We did the best we could. Cooking fires were lit and the food stores we found in the captain's cottage were passed out along with our dried fish. Soon we were grinding grain and cooking flatbread.

After a while we settled into a routine. The hungry men lined up in front of the three cooking fires we had going just outside the entrance to one of the slave barns. As each flatbread came off the fire, it was handed to the next man in line, along with a two dried fish. He then took his food and walked back into the slave barn to the end of the line to repeat the process. This continued all night long, by the light of the moon and the cooking fires, until every man had gone through the line at least four times and some many more.

The men doing the cooking and grain grinding came from the first men we released. They worked quite gladly, and well they should under the circumstances. They sat next to the cooking fires to stay warm and took fresh bread and fish for themselves as they worked and provided food to the others. We never did find the missing slave drivers. They must have scurried from the tunnel under the cover of darkness.

It was just as well the slavers ran. The slaves were getting stronger and stronger by the hour, and, if half the stories I had heard in the past few hours were true, they probably would have torn the slavers to pieces. If they had been taken alive, my archers and I probably would have chopped the bastards down ourselves.

We pulled the bodies of the dead men into one of the slave barns and burned it down as we were leaving two days later. The men that still were not strong enough to walk were placed in the wains, along with what was left of the food. We could not wait any longer to leave or we would not have enough food to reach Restormel.

Chapter Eight

Love and justice.

Becky and I were devastated. We had waved enthusiastically when we saw George ride into Penzance with all those wretched men, and he had smiled and waved back most friendly. But then Becky and I and Mum and Da were in the wain, and the Bishop's men were getting ready to start for Restormel without George. He was still just standing there. He was obviously not coming with us. We looked at each other. Why is that? Does not he live at Restormel with his sisters?

"I thought he was coming with us," Becky said when I asked her what she thought.

"Well, he is standing over there talking to those archers," I said. "Let's climb down and go ask him." And so we did, even though our mum called out to us to come back because it was time to go.

"Hello, Sergeant George. Are you not coming to Restormel with us?"

"Hello yourself, Beth, and you too, Becky. I am not heading for Restormel yet, I am sorry to say. Things have changed as they always seem to do.

"Now I am to wait here in Penzance for two or three weeks until a replacement sergeant can be sent to make sure the food is being properly given out and the work is being done proper in return. But I will be there sooner or later."

Then he said something that sent the girl's hopes soaring.

"I hope I see you when I arrive. And I think I will because my uncle just told me you will be helping my mums take care of my little sisters. Is that true? I hope it is."

"It is, George, it is; or, at least, we think so and hope so. At least that is what we have been told." *He hopes to see us. Mums? Did he say mums?*

****** *Thomas*

George's absence was quickly noticed when I returned to Restormel with George's archers and the surviving slaves. I had some explaining to do to my brother.

"I had to leave George in Penzance because we need a sergeant there to make sure everything is done proper," I told William. "I wanted to leave some of the archers with George but I could not, because I needed every one of them to help bring the slaves here."

William does not need to know I left George there to be learnt more about women and neither do his stepmothers. That would be my secret and Mary's too.

"George is fine, William, but what do you think we should tell the King about his mine and the slaves and about George and his men killing some of the slave drivers? Or should we just ignore what we know about the slaves and mines and see what happens?" *I was changing the subject.*

"It is probably best that we not do anything at the moment, my dear priestly brother," William said to me. "I think we need to send out more parties of archers to see what is happening at the other mines before we make any decisions about what to tell the King."

I agreed with William and told him as much.

"You are right and we should do it soon before it gets any colder. But they had better not be finding any more slaves or serfs, or there is going to be big trouble.

As you might recall, it was right here at Restormel where I told the tin miners to free their slaves and turn them and their serfs into churls with their own gardens and such.

"Right here sitting at this table is where I met with the miners," I said to William as I poked my long finger on the table top so hard that it made a little drumming sound.

"It was right after we took the castle and our galleys were still in Falmouth Harbour. You were not here when the miners came to visit because you had gone off on your horse with George to tell Harold to move our galleys over here to the Fowey."

And on the way you stopped at Trematon to visit Edmund's widow and children. That was before FitzCount and his newly arrived Normans came from Launceston and slaughtered them and then tried to murder you.

****** *Thomas*

Seven grim-faced, three stripe sergeants, every man a long-serving veteran, gathered around to get their orders and learn about the experiences of George and his men at Lannwenep. They had seen the sad state of the slaves George's men and I had brought in; they were not in a good mood.

One of our archers had recognized a man that been taken from his home village as a slave, and the word had spread. William and his other lieutenants and I pretended not to hear the angry words spoken by our men about the King and their treasonous suggestions as to what should happen to him.

It might be acceptable for heathens and captured foreign soldiers to be held as slaves in England, but never an Englishman taken from his own village, not by the King nor anyone else.

We had learnt from my nephew's experiences and proceeded accordingly. This time all but one of the sergeants going out to inspect a mine took eighteen archers with him plus a wain full of food and an outrider with two good horses to come back quickly and tell us if he needed more food or reinforcements. The seventh sergeant took thirty men and three wains of food to the big tin refinery and mine at Truro.

The seven sergeants had listened intently as John Short told them in great detail how George and he and their men had gotten to Lannwenep and what they had seen and done. The sergeants had nodded appreciatively and growled their approval when John described how George had stood up to the mine captain and killed him on the spot. They had growled their appreciation again when John described how he and Edward had killed the other two and told them how George had organized the freeing and feeding of the slaves.

Good! It would soon get around about George being willing to stand up and lead his men in a fight. It would make it much easier for the archers to accept the boys as sergeants.

"George and John did exactly the right thing," William told the sergeants.

"And so did Edward. Our response to finding slaves on our lands will always be the same as if we find them on Moorish galleys—we free them and feed them. The only difference is, instead of killing them outright the way we do pirates by tossing them over the side, those of the slavers who survive are to be brought back to here or Cyprus for judging—and hanging or chopping it they are guilty."

There were a lot of questions and rightly so.

"Yes, Ralph, we are also freeing the serfs at the mines and refinerie as well, even if it means fighting. Bring them all with you when you return—and their families too. And tell them they can come here and work for their food and shelter as free men if they have a mind.

"Yes, that is it exactly; you are only to leave the mine captains and their overseers who have not acted as slave drivers and used their men as slaves. Also, you are to leave behind any serfs or churls who do not want to stop working at the mine even after they know they are free.

"Yes, you may do as George and John did—kill anyone who tries to stop you from freeing the miners and their families. No man can go wrong if he fights to free them.

"Yes, you are exactly right, Tom. If there is any doubt about their innocence, you are to bring the overseers you take alive here to Restormel for judging. One reason you have all been given more men than George and John is so any slavers you find who have tortured and starved their slaves and serfs will not be able to get away in the confusion."

William and I are death on anyone that mistreats their serfs and slaves, just as we are on churchmen that take advantage of their believers. It made us think of the way we and our mum were treated when we were lads, and we did not like it. It pleased us to free them and judge their abusers.

What mostly worried us, however, was not knowing what the King and his chancellor and justiciar would say and do when they found out the King's slaves and serfs had run with our help and his mines were no longer producing.

******

George rode in over the Restormel drawbridge and clattered into the bailey two weeks and two days after I left Penzance with the girls, their parents, and the slaves he and his men had freed. He came in with the file of horse archers I had sent to Penzance with a horse for him to ride.

Of course, I sent some of Raymond's men to bring George in. I wanted to make sure he was not attacked by robbers on the road, as is often the fate of single travelers.

It had been a most interesting two weeks whilst George was still away in Penzance with Mary. One after another our mine inspection sergeants returned. Three of the seven brought in the mine captains and their slave drivers in chains, and every one of the sergeants was accompanied by newly freed serfs and slaves. Several brought in hungry free people, as well. Only two of the King's seven mines and his Truro tin refinery were in operation when they left, and how long the refinery would continue to produce white tin for coins seemed questionable, even if the King's other mines were somehow restarted.

Andrew, who was once a cartwright's apprentice and made his mark on our articles as Andrew Cartwright, was the sergeant who took thirty men and famine food to the Truro mine and refinery. He found only free men at Truro but also a possible solution to what could be a big problem for us.

It seemed the captain at Truro did not think his refinery would be able to operate much longer, because the shortage of nearby trees for wood to burn meant the charcoal the refinery required to heat the ore was beginning to cost more coins than was being fetched by the resulting tin.

What Andrew discovered was that the captain at Truro was quite worried about what the King and his chancellor would do to him when they heard there would be no more tin revenues for the King because of the shortage of wood to burn.

At the time, neither Andrew nor the captain knew the day of reckoning was even closer to hand because most of the mines that had been supplying him with raw and partially processed ore had just been shut down by the loss of their slaves and serfs.

I questioned Andrew closely and decided to go to Truro for a visit to see for myself how the refining was done and confirm what Andrew told us. Why? Because with a few coins for the Truro captain, we might be able to blame the King's loss of his tin revenues on the shortage of wood for charcoal instead of our freeing of the mines' serfs and slaves and our topping of their drivers.

****** *Thomas*

William convened a court of sergeants each time one of our mine inspection parties returned with slavers. The sergeants took it quite seriously, as well they might, since most of them started life as village lads and many had been serfs or slaves at one time or another. They lined up the mine's English serfs and slaves and questioned them closely as to how they had been treated. A few of the slave drivers were released when their former slaves and serfs spoke well of them. The rest were dragged weeping and begging and promising to change to a gallows the archers erected near the camp.

My brother does not like men that mistreat slaves and serfs and their families, does he? He kicked the stool out from under them himself and spit on them when he did. It was no wonder our archers and sailors both adore and fear their captain.

By the time the sergeants' courts finished their work, Cornwall had, to the best of our knowledge, no serfs or slaves other than those at the monasteries where we had as yet made no real effort to free them. The only exception was here at Launceston where the nearby St. Stephen's Monastery now had no slaves or serfs.

As it turned out, we did not have to do much to get the monks at St. Stephen's to come to Jesus and free their slaves and serfs. The abbot had heard about the fates of the Penzance priest and the slave drivers and serf drivers. He quickly freed those at his monastery. We know because five of them promptly walked to Restormel with their families and signed on to work for us.

******

The slaves and serfs we freed from the King's mines followed the usual pattern for such men—some stayed to work for us as free men, some left to try to return home, and some died and had to be buried. Initially, we had just under four hundred former mining slaves and serfs in our camp.

In addition, almost two hundred of them left to try to return to their home villages and countries as soon as they regained their strength. We let them go and carried them on our cogs and galleys whenever they were going in the direction they wanted to travel. William even gave the poor sods some dried fish and a few copper coins to help them on their way.

Others of the men we freed, perhaps most of them, had no homes left to that they could return. We let them stay with us as free men in exchange for their labour when they got strong enough to work.

It was clear to William and me, however, that for one reason or another most of those who stayed would not become strong enough in time to pull an oar for the Company in the attack we hope to launch against the French. As a result, we concentrated on finding men from the surrounding villages who would help us row in exchange for a few coins and the promise of a share of any prize money that came our way.

1451 | 9781520285795 | 1451

Location: B5

VOM.GFI

Title:	Castling The King Action and Adventure - a medieval saga set in feudal England about an Englishman who rose in the years of turmoil leading up to the Magna Carta (The Company of Archers)
Cond:	Good
ser:	vo_list
tation:	Workstation-01
ate:	2021-06-14 18:53:08 (UTC)
ccount:	Veteran-Outsource
rig Loc:	B5
SKU:	VOM GFI
eq#:	1451
uickPick	R04
nit_id	2172329
idth	0.72 in
ank	4,444,344

delist unit# 2172329

XXXXX

Almost every evening, William and I talked about where we might find more rowers and apprentice archers. We even talked about visiting the monasteries to recruit their slaves and serfs "to fight for the King" and tried to guess how many men we would get. But it was only talk.

Each time we talked, we decided to wait until we knew how the King would react to the parchment which we wrote for the Truro captain sent to him explaining how the famine had caused the miners to flee from some of the mines in order to search for food, and informing him some of them had enrolled as sailors to help him fight the French and rebel barons. It also mentioned that the mines were becoming exhausted and there was a shortage of wood to burn to cook the ore.

What I somehow "forgot "to mention in the parchment I scribed for the Truro captain to send to the King was how we caused closure of his mines by freeing the men that were being kept as slaves and hanging the slavers that had been mistreating them. The parchment also did not mention the coins and employment the King's captain at Truro received for sending the parchment.

What I thought about doing, but never did, was putting on my bishop's robe and mitre and visiting

Bodmin Monastery and the chapter house at Crantock to see if I could order their abbots to do the right thing and free their serfs and slaves "as the Pope has ordered." I was tempted to do so because, almost certainly, some of the men they freed would come to us for employment and be strong enough to pull an oar.

Bodmin would have certainly been the best place to start. It was the biggest of the monasteries in Cornwall, and it certainly had the most serfs and slaves being used as farmers and servants—over one hundred, I had been told.

What I finally ended up doing was a mistake. I had William send a parchment to the King suggesting that he order the abbots to send their serfs and slaves to us to help during the coming war. I did that so the Church would be pissed at King John for losing them and not at me or William. Nothing ever came of it. The Pope's nuncio probably talked him out of it.

****** *Beth*

Becky and I certainly learnt a lot from George's mums in the weeks that followed our arrival at Restormel—about George and his family and about babies and what pleasures men. It was quite exciting, what we learnt about caring for men and making babies, I mean.

I know it was hard to believe, but George's father was an earl—whatever an earl is—and was once a serf and even lower than us. But he had raised himself by becoming an archer and knowing how to put his feet down to the beat of a marching drum. At least that is what Helen and Anne and Tori told us.

What was most surprising was to discover that George really was a priest and could say the words in church-talk and pray at people, but that it did not matter because the Pope allows priests such as George and his father to marry and have more than one wife if they marry sisters.

My mum did not believe it at first, about priests like George being able to marry sisters, even though Beth and I told her we thought it was a wonderful idea. Mum does now, because before she and Da went back to Penzance to get his tools and her loom, the Bishop himself happened to see her at the cook tent and told her it was true. He even blessed her and let her kiss his ring to keep poxes away.

Chapter Nine

Thomas goes to Windsor.

After a long, hard ride I arrived in Windsor with my arse aching. And once again I stayed at the priest's cottage and the men with me, my four archer escorts this time, moved into his barn with their horses. I stayed there even though the priest charged me much too much for each of us getting a supper of lamb stew with a fresh loaf and a slice of cheese in the morning.

Before I left for Windsor, I had checked with William and Peter and to see if there had been word from our spies at Exeter, or from anyone else, regarding the French or the rebel barons. There was not. All we knew for sure from our spies at Rougemont was that the Earl of Devon was still in France, and his wife and daughters thought he and his fellow barons were meeting with Phillip to offer him the English crown.

According to the castle servants, the Earl had the sailors' pox and was searching for both a cure and a village infant his wife could pretend to birth as his son and heir. His wife and the servants think he intends to bring one back from France and claim it is his.

That there was no news about the barons or a French invasion was to be expected; it was still early days. The French king and his son, Louis, who commanded his army, would not start gathering his men until the spring when the leaves begin to spring up once again from the trees that were dead all winter. And even then he might decide to wait even longer until the spring planting was finished.

Information as to the intentions of the barons and King Phillip was no better at Windsor than it was in Cornwall. Neither the priest of Windsor's parish church, with whom I had a long discussion, nor anyone I talked to in the King's court seemed to know anything about anything. If they did, they certainly were not telling me.

The Windsor priest, at least, had commented on the famine. He had been praying, he told me, for the farm labourers in his parish and their families because they were starving.

Praying was all he could do for the serfs and churls, he had explained with a question in his voice as if he hoped I would agree, "because the poor are always with us." I merely made a grunting sound for him to take as agreeing or not agreeing as he wished.

About the barons and France and the possibility of war, neither the priest nor the courtiers had heard anything. The priest's housekeeper was obviously his wife even though it was forbidden by the Church. She said nothing to me during my entire stay, not a single word. She and her children did not take their meals with us.

Father Rufus was the priest. He once again revealed rather arrogantly, forgetting that he had also told me the same thing each of the two previous times I had had a bed off him, that he is the third son of a minor lord named Brereton with a manor near Chester that had a moat so foul that fish could not live in it. He was quite proud of having learnt enough Latin and prayers at the Priory of Saint Frideswide to be ordained without ever having to read the Bible. He bought his copy from a poor scribe, he told me. Oxford is full of them.

Rufus had seemed quite astonished during my first visit some years ago to hear I had been born a serf and become a bishop. He had questioned me closely at the time as to how I had done it and seemed quite dejected when I said I had risen in the Church the traditional way—by bribing the papal nuncio. He must have finally remembered I had stayed with him previously; this time, for the first time, he did not mention where he was birthed.

I have been here at Windsor all day waiting for the King and William Marshal to appear. It was damn uncomfortable and quite boring despite all the meaningless personal gossip I have been hearing from the King's toadies and all the other waiting petitioners.

As far as I can tell, no word has yet reached the King's court about the King putting his seal on the mercenary-like contracts I scribed to permanently give William and his heirs Exeter and Rougemont Castle and its manors as freeholds in exchange for a few coins and Cornwall's support for the King against the French and the rebel barons.

I can only conclude, since everyone here talks and gossips about everything and everyone, that it is likely the King's men and his courtiers know nothing about the parchment that would grant us Rougemont and no more than I do about the plans of King John and William Marshal or those of the French King and the rebel barons.

Could it be King John and his men know the French and barons are *not* coming? That is certainly one of the questions I intend to put directly to William Marshal if I ever have an opportunity to speak with him privately. If anyone would know about the French and barons, it would be Sir William. He and the King surely have spies in Phillip's court. *And once again I wondered if they had any in Cornwall and Devon and who they might be.*

Or could it be the King has not signed the parchment because he is upset with us about his mines being closed? No, probably not, or the gossips would have said something about it and demanded an explanation. It was more likely the greedy sod wants more coins as well as our loyalty and blood. A demand for more coins is what I expect and why I brought them.

Ah well, there is nothing to be accomplished by constantly worrying about such things. All I can do is wait here at court for Sir William to arrive and then, if I can get a private word with him, ask him what he knows about the French and barons and if the King intends to put his seal to the parchments.

****** *Thomas*

It should not be much longer before the King and Sir William arrive. One of the servants I sat next to in the court jakes about an hour ago assured me they were hunting in the forest and usually returned to court about this time each day.

Having a covered jakes, where visitors and members of the court can shite or piss at Windsor without being wetted by the rain, is a great improvement over what it used to be when Richard was king and all one could do is find a quiet room or a tree. At least, I think so.

One of the few interesting things I heard as I waited was several courtiers openly complaining about the King's latest scutage for those that do not bring their men in to join the King's army in the spring. It was interesting to hear because one of the men complaining the loudest was not on the parchment William Marshal had sent me listing the barons who were thought to be disloyal to the King.

About the only other interesting thing was what I heard from the King's courtiers about the famine that had England in its deadly grip—absolutely nothing. The famine did not seem to concern them. They were obviously interested in other more significant matters, such as the time left on the Queen's pregnancy and the number of buttons on the Queen's gown and what the number of buttons portends, a subject I heard extensively discussed and was twice asked for my opinion.

******

I was close to starving when the King finally arrived. Sir William Marshal was with him and so was his pregnant Queen wearing all her buttons. John entered the hall with his Queen on his arm and accompanied by a great entourage of knights and clerics, including the Duke of Sussex and several other important nobles.

There was immediately a great bustling and moving about as everyone, including me, moved towards them with lots of bowing and scraping and the holding out of petitions. Almost at the same moment, several fashionably dressed ladies suddenly appeared among us as if they had been conjured up by a magician.

Nothing happened. The King and Queen and Sir William and their companions exchanged bows and pleasantries with various petitioners and courtiers.

A few minutes later, despite the chill of the day, the royals wandered outside on to the grassy area on the north side of the castle's bailey with a great gaggle of fawning courtiers and clerics following close behind them. I, of course, went out after them along with everyone else. *What else could I do?*

After a while, Sir William pretended he had just seen me and he and a man I did not recognize walked over to speak with me. Sir William named the other man as Walter DeGray, as if I was somehow expected to know of him and be impressed. So I bowed profusely and acted as if I was quite impressed and honoured. I had never heard of the man.

We talked about the French and the rebellious barons. The two King's men seemed unconcerned that we might be overheard by the people standing around us. We also talked about where the coming war might be fought and my petition to the King for Rougemont Castle and Devon's lands.

The two men agreed the French were coming and some of the English and Welsh barons would join them and so, perhaps, would some Scots. Their spies at Phillip's court have confirmed it. *Scots helping an English king? That is something new; perhaps they are not as canny as I had been led to believe.*

So why did you not send a galloper with a parchment informing us? I wondered, but did not ask. I did not ask because I was sure I knew the answer—we in Cornwall were too insignificant compared to the great and mighty that gossiped at the King's court.

Then Sir William caused me to temporarily lose my breath and my thoughts.

"They are almost certainly coming, and the King thinks you should pay more for the freehold of Rougemont since your brother the Earl will not be contributing knights or soldiers to the King's army, just sailors and shipping. You and your brother will have to find the coins if you want Rougemont because the King needs more money so he can hire mercenaries."

I pretended to be undone by his remarks, but then I rallied.

"That is most unfortunate, Sir William, but perhaps understandable given the King's great desire to defeat them and the sad fact of Cornwall having no knights or men-at-arms to contribute to the effort.

"How much would it take to satisfy the King so he puts his mark and his seal on the parchments and I can take them with me back to Cornwall?"

Does he think we can pay more because he knows of our treasure? It surely cannot be because he thinks Cornwall's lands have large revenues.

"Forty pounds would be sufficient," said Walter DeGray rather promptly.

"Forty pounds?" I exclaimed. *Is that all? I have got more than that in my money belt.*

"In the name of God," I said. "That is a lot for Cornwall to raise, being as there is a great famine on the land and there are no manors in Cornwall since it cannot support a single knight even in the best of times."

I gave the two men my most sincere, depressed look and then suddenly brightened up considerably.

"Wait a minute. Yes; now, I remember. We just carried a valuable cargo into London for the Greek merchants that have been supplying the crusaders. They have sent in some of the flower paste that is so valuable and easily sold because it makes the pain of a soldier's wound go away.

"There is a moneylender in London that has agreed to advance us enough coins to pay for the cargo. I am supposed to borrow the necessary coins and use them to pay the Greeks and buy the paste before I return to Cornwall. But the Greeks can wait, since the King obviously comes first. Yes, they could." *There are no Greeks; I have got more than that with me.*

We talked and argued and negotiated as I tried desperately to get them to accept fewer coins for the King. It was what they would expect me to do and what I want them to report to the King—that Cornwall is too poor to support even a single knight, let alone one of his court favourites.

Finally, we reached an agreement on a lower price. It happened after Marshal admitted he had not received any news as to when and where the French would attack. Even worse for Cornwall, he also admitted that even if we paid the required coins we would still have to wait to take Rougemont until the fighting actually began to be absolutely sure Devon was against the King.

They seem to think the uncertainty as to when the fighting would start would be a problem for us because it always was for the Cinque Ports of Kent and Sussex. Those are the ports that must provide the King with shipping for fourteen days each year in lieu of paying taxes. Obviously neither Sir William nor DeGray knew we intended to start the fighting as soon as the French fleet was assembled.

"Let me be sure I clearly understand what you are proposing on behalf of the King, Sir William. If I go to the London moneylenders and bring thirty-two pounds of silver coins here for the King the day after tomorrow, instead of using it to buy the flower paste, I would receive the parchments signed and sealed and ready to be placed in the parish records?"

Marshal and DeGray both nodded.

"Well then, your word is certainly good enough for me. I will leave for London immediately and try to get the necessary coins from the moneylenders. I am quite optimistic even though I certainly cannot promise them. Hopefully, I will see you here the day after tomorrow. If not, I will send you a parchment message so you will at least know I tried."

Damn. Now I will have to go to London and come back, if only for the sake of appearing to tell the truth. Oh well, at least it does not look like rain. Besides, I surely do like the drink the alewife at the White Horse brews with wine and juniper berries.

******

Two days later and I was newly returned to Windsor after riding all day on a bouncing horse cart with a terrible headache from drinking too much juniper-flavoured brew at the White Horse.

I paid one of the Windsor guards to carry a message into William Marshal. Then I sat on a bench and held my head until he and Walter DeGray walked up to me.

"How did it go?" DeGray asked. "Do you fetch the coins?"

"It went well for the coins; not so well for my drinking jenever in London last night and having to spend all day getting here on a horse cart that somehow found every hole on the King's road. My head hurts most terrible," I said mournfully.

"Jenever? I have never heard of it. What is it?" asked DeGray with a smile at my obvious discomfort. *The sod.*

I wonder if DeGray is smiling because my head hurts and he is a right bastard, or because I have got the coins and he is a King's man and is going to end up with some of them. Probably both.

"Comes from cooking wine with the juice of juniper berries and then letting it bubble in the pot, so they say. Strong is what it is. Really strong. An alewife in a tavern near where I stay in London brews it."

"Well, you fetched the coins and that is what is important. Come with us to my room so we can count them and give you the parchments on which the king has made his mark and seal. We want to talk about the French and the barons."

* * * * * *

An hour later, my purse was lighter, I had the signed and sealed parchments in a leather messenger tube slung over my shoulder, and I was back with my men that had been waiting outside the castle entrance. They were sheltering from the cold rain that was lightly falling by huddling under the horse cart I had rented. I was anxious to get back to Cornwall and so were my men. We would leave our horses in London and return on a Company galley that was presently loading passengers and cargo for a long run out to the Holy Land.

I thought about what Marshal and DeGray had told me as we walked back to the rectory. There was no doubt about it according to the King's two men. Devon and his fellow barons offered the English crown to Phillip of France, and he has accepted their offer.

The French, they said, would assemble their army after the spring planting is finished and sail for England to join up with Devon and the rest of the traitorous barons. They claimed to have no idea at all where the French would land.

Two hours later, my men and I were bouncing along the King's road towards London in our rented horse cart. We had just hit a particularly large hole when it suddenly struck me that Marshal and DeGray had mentioned neither the great famine nor the missing slaves nor the closing of most of the King's tin mines in Cornwall.

Is it possible the king does not yet know? Or does he know and not care because defeating his rebel barons and the French is more important?

Chapter Ten

The spies.

Sea birds poking at the sand along the French shoreline took to the air as the battered, old fishing boat nosed onto the rock-strewn strand at Honfleur. It was just before high tide on a cold, windy, early spring day. It was still stormy in the channel, and it had been a long, rough voyage. The strand smelled of seaweed and dead fish as strands usually do.

Two of the four crudely dressed fishermen on board the boat immediately jumped down onto the beach and began to pull the boat as far as possible out of the water. They did so because they did not want to chance it drifting away if the tide continued to rise. They were experienced sailors, but the waves in the channel had been more than a little difficult and they were glad to be ashore.

Another old and battered fishing boat, similar to the first, came in immediately behind with two more fishermen and a middle-aged couple on board. The two fishermen that had pulled the first boat ashore also pulled the second boat ashore. Then they held up their hands to the couple to help them step down on to the damp and rocky strand.

It was good that they offered to help them, for both the man and woman were not experienced sailors and had been almost constantly sea poxed during the trip from Cornwall. They were both more than a little weak in the legs and a few pound lighter. The man's tunic and cap marked him as a moderately successful merchant.

All around the two newly arrived fishing boats were similar old wooden boats and dinghies in various conditions and states of repair. Many were turned upside down to keep out the rain—because their owners lived in them when they were not fishing.

Only if a would-be thief or robber was totally unaware of what would happen next would he try to take the merchant's coin pouch. That is when, in the final seconds of his life, he had discover the man's tunic covered a shirt of chain mail and a carefully concealed two-edged short sword. His wife was dressed as the wife of a somewhat successful merchant would be dressed and had a similar coin pouch and knife under her skirts.

The man was Henry, once a crusader and a Moorish galley slave, and, until recently, the lieutenant commanding all of the land forces of the Company of archers. The woman by his side was his new wife, Jeanette, the spy the captain of the Company had once placed in the crusader camp across the waterway from Constantinople's walls.

All six of the men with Henry and Jeanette were sergeants or chosen men from the Cornwall camp of the Company of Archers. They were the best swordsmen among the available archers who could speak passable French and might be able to sail a fishing boat back and forth between France and Cornwall to carry messages.

******

Thomas and I had tried to talk Henry out of going to Honfleur with Jeanette but he had been adamant.

"Let Peter take over the land fighting," Henry had said with the relaxed smile of a man whose mind was made up. "He is better than I am at training the men and leading them in battle, and we all know it. I am ready to settle down with Jeanette, enjoy life as a French tavern owner, and be a spy for a while."

Henry had made a decision and there was no changing it.

"Besides," Henry said, "I was born in Calais and lived there until I went for a soldier. So I know the language and have an accent the French soldiers and sailors will believe."

There was, of course, a slight problem at the time. Henry was not in France and we did not have a sailors' tavern for Henry and Jeanette to operate. We also did not know where they might find one that would be frequented by the sailors that would be in the French invasion fleet or how much they might have to pay to buy it.

The only thing certain was our need to move quickly, that meant Henry and Jeanette would probably have to pay much too much for whatever tavern or other business they bought. That is why they carried so many gold and silver coins in their purses. The coins should be safe, because the group was well armed. The raggedy roll of dirty bedding two of the fishermen were carrying over their shoulders had three swords wrapped in it.

In addition to the short sword hidden under Henry's jacket, each of them, including Jeanette, also carried a deadly fisherman's knife.

******

Except for a few friendly nods from fishermen working or living on their boats, the merchant and his wife and their two roughly dressed companions did not attract much attention as they walked towards the crude, wooden buildings where the local fishermen sold their catches to the Paris buyers and took their pleasures with wine and women. The other four "fishermen" remained behind to guard the boats and be ready to push them into the water and sail to Cornwall on a moment's notice.

The couple's plan was quite simple: find a place to eat and sleep and then look for a waterfront tavern or market stall patronized by sailors and pay whatever it takes to buy it. Then the listening would begin. Anything important they heard would be carried back to Cornwall on one or both of the fishing boats.

An exhausted Henry and his woman rented a bed for the night in one of the waterfront taverns. The two fishermen bunked in another bed nearby. Then the couple and the two fishermen drank and ate in different places and spent the rest of that day and all the next wandering about the port to get the lay of the land.

It took several days and a number of discrete and tentative inquiries to find a place that might meet their needs. It was the two fishermen who found it.

The newlyweds had something to eat and went to bed early to recover from their exhausting trip. The two fishermen, on the other hand, were excited to be in the land of their parents for the first time in their lives, though they would claim to be from an isolated Norman village if anyone were to ask.

The two men posed as brothers. They visited a number of the local taverns and bemoaned their fate over their bowls of wine, implying that one of them had personal problems involving a woman in the small Norman port where they had previously fished.

It meant, they sadly implied, that they could not go back for a while. They had decided as a result, they confided to the barmaids and other patrons as they drank their wine, to change their lives by becoming sailors and seeing the world instead of repairing their old boat and returning to fishing.

"If we cannot find berths as sailors on a cog or ship heading to someplace warm, we will just have to stay here and try to replace enough of the rotted wood on our boat so we can fish around here until something turns up. Where do you think we should ask around about becoming sailors?" they inquired of everyone.

What the two men discovered and reported to the newlyweds the next morning was that the taverns frequented by the sailors and shipping owners were not those where the fishermen got together to drink. The sailors' haunts were further down the beach, nearer to Honfleur's wharves and warehouses. They were given the names of several of the sailors' taverns and directions as to how to find them.

Later in the morning, the middle-aged couple and their two "sons" walked together along the shore to the area of the wharves. Late in the afternoon, they struck gold at the third tavern they visited. It was already full of sailors from the cargo transports tied along the wharves and at anchor in the harbour.

Henry inquired of the owner when the wine was served and was told he was not available. The owner's woman, the tavern girl sadly reported, was down once again with the sailors' pox and probably would not survive this time.

Such a pity, everyone agreed, and one of the sergeants knocked three times on the wooden table for good luck and whispered a silent prayer under his breath.

******

"There are cures in Rome if you have enough coins to pay for the prayers needed to go with them. I know because I have been there and seen them work for both men and women."

That was the lie Henry told the gaunt, white-haired man who greeted them when he and Jeanette knocked softly on the door to his sleeping room above the tavern's hall. *It was not true; he had never been to Rome.*

"And God must want her cured, for he sent me and my wife and sons here looking for a tavern to buy with the coins you will need to get her cured and live rich forever after."

"Our boys are fishermen, and we want to get them ashore where it is safer," Jeanette explained.

After two hours of intense hand waving and beard stroking negotiations, Henry and the tavern owner made their marks on a parchment drafted by a hastily summoned scrivener. It resulted in a substantial number of gold bezants and other coins changing hands—so many, the tavern owner probably would have sold even if his woman had not been poxed and needed the curing that can only be found where the Pope lives.

****** *Jeanette*

My husband's new tavern was a splendid place with old, blackened roof timbers. It had a fireplace at one end of the drinking hall and eight long, wooden tables and benches on a dirt floor that soaked up spilled drinks and such. Its biggest problem, as we soon came to discover, was its fireplace. It sometimes poured smoke into the room because it did not draw properly. On the other hand, it does keep the chill off the room and our customers seem to like it. They say all the smoke in the room and the warmth of the fire reminds them of how they lived with their families as boys before they went to sea.

We took over the tavern quite smoothly because both of the barmaids and the cook agreed to remain with us on the same terms they had previously enjoyed. Our two "sons" were helpful as well. They made themselves useful when drunken customers needed assistance in resolving their disputes and by taking over the dipping of wine out of the barrels late in the evening after Henry and I went off to bed.

Most important of all, our tavern was a popular place and so well located it was usually full of seamen, merchants serving the port's shipping, and even customs officials. We actually earned quite a few coins each day and certainly heard a lot of talk about the port and the shipping trade.

Everything almost changed one cold, rainy morning about a week after we bought the place. Three tough-looking men came in when I finally unbarred the door to their insistent pounding. They immediately demanded bowls of wine and then informed me they would not be paying for it because they were there to collect the weekly fee we were required to pay for their protection and good will, and free wine is part of the fee. We had been expecting them ever since we bought the place.

"Oh, I see," I said to the man that announced their demands to me as I motioned for Henry to come join us. "Well, you need to speak with my husband, do you not? He is the new owner, and I am sure he would like to talk with you."

The tough-looking man that was obviously the leader of the three men greeted Henry in a most unfriendly manner and welcomed him to Honfleur. The other two stood back and did their best to appear intimidating and ferocious.

He and his men, the unfriendly man explained, were the watchmen that protected all the quayside taverns and merchants from trouble after the city gates closed and the regular city watch disappeared. They were calling to collect their weekly fee.

Henry and I had our first disagreement when I suggested we should temporarily pay the local protection pirates whatever they ask in order to avoid attracting attention. We would not be here long anyway, I said.

Henry refused. "It is not in my nature," he explained. "What if it became known to the archers that I had let such wankers threaten me into doing what they wanted? I would never live it down."

At first, Henry and I played the role of simple merchant folk and went along with the fee collectors, asking them about their fees and their services and such and making up stories about our experiences running a tavern in Normandy. The three men were quite full of themselves and soon began increasing their efforts to intimidate us with various warnings about fire setters and a timid city watch that never comes outside the walls after the city gates are shut and such.

They were so sure of themselves and concentrated so hard on intimidating Henry and me that they did not pay much attention when our two guards quietly told an early-arriving sailor he would have to leave as we were still closed.

It was not until our visitors heard the loud *thunk* as the heavy wooden bar dropped into place sealing the door that they realized the place was empty except for the seven of us. The barring of the door seemed to encourage them even more since they apparently thought it meant *we* could not get away.

"And who besides you three would we have protecting us if we pay you?" Henry inquired rather politely as one of the men brought out a knife and began paring his fingernails with it.

"Three's enough, old man. Three's enough."

That was the wrong thing to say to my new husband; that I knew for sure. He was sensitive man, you see.

"Oh, I am sure it is," Henry said as he brought his two-edged sword up from the bench behind the table and sliced it straight into the man's face with a heavy, two-handed swing.

"But what if there are only two of you?" he asked with a snarl.

******

The other two toughs stood there gobsmacked for a moment as their spokesman went backwards from the strike, the edge of Henry's blade stuck deep in his skull. They turned and ran for the door as Henry wrenched the blade free with a grunt. They did not make it. Our two "sons" cut them down before they reached it.

One of the men squealed for a moment on his hands and knees until the heavy *splat* of another fierce blow cut off the noise and most of his head.

My husband and I looked at each other.

"What now, husband?" I said rather blandly with a sweet smile as I cocked my head inquiringly even though my heart was racing. "It is not good for our turnover to have dead men bleeding on the floor whilst we are handing out bowls."

Henry smiled his approval at the mildness of my comment and then nodded his satisfaction quite strongly towards the two sergeants to acknowledge their assistance in handling our would-be protectors.

"Pull the bastards out the back door if no one is around and cover them with firewood or something," Henry ordered them. "We will carry them down to the boats when it gets dark and take them for a swim. But first bring in some wood for the fire and get it going; it looks to be another cold and nasty day."

******

Three days later, our tavern was suddenly full of talk and rumours that King Phillip was about to call for all the fishing boats and shipping along the coast to be assembled for the use of his army. Where they would assemble and whether or not the rumour was true were all hotly argued. It was all everyone could talk about.

Henry and I and our sons fetched many a bowl of wine in the several days that followed as we asked questions about the rumours and agreed with all the answers, as any good tavern owner would do. We debated sending word to Cornwall. I wanted us all to go, but we did not because Henry decided we still did not know enough.

Chapter Eleven

A gathering of archers.

Henry and Jeanette were not the only ones making progress that winter. My brother Thomas returned from London on one of our galleys with the King's seal on the parchments he had drafted. All winter long, galleys and cogs fought their way through the Atlantic and channel storms, coming in constantly from the east with exhausted men and additional famine supplies.

The arrival of our boats and the additional men and supplies presented us with several pleasant problems—where to moor our boats and what to do with the men and supplies. It kept Peter Sergeant, the lieutenant who had replaced Henry, and the rest of us constantly scrambling to organize and accommodate the new arrivals and the food distributed to those who needed it most.

The result was an ever-growing number of otherwise-idle archers and sailors camped and training along the river where some of the galleys had been pulled out of the water and at Fowey Village at the mouth of the river. The sailors were kept busy working on their boats and learning to fight with swords and pikes; the archers with practicing with their archery and land fighting.

******

Fowey Village and its harbour were where Harold spent the winter—intensively training our men how to fight at sea, with particular emphasis on using our archers and sailors to take cargo transports and galleys and sail away with them as prizes.

My son George became Harold's apprentice sergeant and followed him about wherever he went. Both of them lived in a hurriedly-built cottage next to the new tent camp Harold set up next Fowey Village.

One of the smith's girls, the older and taller one, went there with George to make sure his clothes were clean and he and Harold were properly fed and such. Her name is Beth. She and George, Thomas told me with a great deal of satisfaction soon after he returned from London, "are off to Fowey Village to help Harold and get to know each other. They are betrothed and I will marry them in the spring and add her sister to our family next year."

It was all quite proper between George and Beth, as Thomas said the necessary words and prayers for them before he rode to London accompanied by six of Raymond's horse archers. I gave George several gifts to celebrate their joining and comfort him when he was away from her bed: a shirt of chain mail to protect him and an absolutely splendid set of carved chess pieces I had bought from one of the Constantinople refugees.

Everyone was quite pleased with the arrangement, particularly Beth and George. Even Helen smiled and said she approved when I asked her about it last night.

"He is grown up to be a man, my love," she explained as she snuggled up against me and nibbled on my ear. "He needs a woman to care for him just as you do."

******

Our training efforts and preparations for war intensified as our galleys and the archers arrived so that we had an ever more powerful force. They intensified again after the King put his seal to the agreement regarding our future ownership of Rougemont and its lands, even though we kept the agreement secret so only Thomas and I knew they would be ours if the Earl of Devon joined the rebel barons.

I do not know what we would have done if the King had not agreed to reward us with Rougemont if we take it—probably nothing different. The Earl of Devon was too much of a threat to us, and the King and his men were far away and nowhere near as strong as they seemed to think. If we ever take Rougemont, we will say our prayers and fight to keep it even if the King tries to take it for himself or tries to give it to one of his favourites.

As you might imagine, word quickly spread through our ranks about the recall of our galleys and fighting men. And, of course, everyone could see the big build-up of our forces and our greatly increased training and preparations.

The men and their sergeants were certain something big was afoot even if they did not know what it was. And what our men knew, their women and the merchants and spies all knew as well.

But only my five lieutenants and their apprentices, if they had one, knew that our plan was to hit the French and barons whilst the French fleet was still assembling. We did not want anyone else to know until after we sailed. That meant the sergeants captaining our galleys would not be told their destinations until all our galleys were in the Fowey estuary and fully loaded and rowing for France under favourable weather conditions.

Preparing our men and galleys for a battle, but not telling them where and when it would be until the last minute worked quite nicely when we attacked Tunis and Algiers; hopefully, it would work here as well. Many of our men were veterans of one or more of our raids. They understood and were quite pleased with the secrecy.

God forbid things change and we have to deploy our men to fight on land because the French and barons steal a march on us and reach Cornwall or Devon before we can attack their fleet. We would fight them on land if they come to Cornwall or Devon, but we would greatly prefer to take the French transports as prizes so that the French never come here at all.

Rumours of all sorts continued to fly among our men. I heard about them all the time. They could not be helped. And if the recall of our archers and the sudden increase in their training and our war preparations had awakened everyone's imaginations, the sudden and unannounced departure of Henry and the arrival of Peter as his replacement lit a fire under them.

Peter, Thomas, Raymond and I had each taken one of Thomas's older boy sergeants for an apprentice sergeant and begun a routine. And so had Randolph who had been promoted to lieutenant and taken Henry's place as the Company's deputy commander. Each day the young apprentice sergeants rode with us as we move up and down the cart path along the Fowey, making sure the archers had their required archery and sword fighting practices, lots of good food, warm clothes, and warm places to sleep.

Our young sergeant apprentices were quite keen and helpful as they fetched and scribed and ran errands for us as we required. Now our senior lieutenants could all make lists and send and receive written reports and orders. Hopefully, the apprentices are learning by watching and listening to us so someday they can take our places. *Even better, Thomas has assigned one of the next-oldest boys to George and each of the other young apprentice sergeants. He has apprenticed them to the older apprentices, so to speak.*

The young lads proved their worth. George and his young helper talked to the arriving sergeant captains and added their galleys and transports and the names of their men to the parchment lists they were keeping for

Harold. That is how we learnt two galleys and a cog full of famine grain were missing and presumed lost with all hands. According to the list, they should have arrived weeks ago.

We did not have a clue as to what happened to our missing men. It was most likely the effect of having to sail in the off-season when the weather is bad or, possibly, pirates in the case of the cog.

****** *William*

Harold was spending all his time in the Fowey Village camp with my son George as his aide and apprentice and an even younger student of Thomas's school as George's helper. They were there to supervise the archers and sailors who, although they did not know it yet, were practicing to fight their way onto the French galleys and cargo transports and sail them away as prizes.

Archers of every rank, including me and my lieutenants so as to set an example, were required to engage in archery and land-fighting practice every day except Sunday, even when we were aboard our galleys and cogs.

Archery and fighting practices when we are aboard our galleys and transports was necessarily limited to small groups of archers. On land, such as where our men now were, it additionally involved entire galley companies of archers and pike men walking in unison on the same foot to the beat of a rowing drum and changing the direction they were marching when the command was given. It was a very useful way to move them about and looked very impressive to those who were watching.

Our archers and sailors are becoming increasingly excited by the assembling of all our men and galleys and their increased training. They think we are preparing them for a big prize-taking raid on some place that has galleys, such as a Moorish port like Algiers, or for an invasion of Moorish Spain, or perhaps Ireland or north to the Swedes.

On the other hand, they know the French and the rebel English barons do not have war galleys, so the only thing that they are certain about is that France and England are not where they will be going to fight.

******

The news that something big was in the wind had reached everyone, even our distant senior sergeants and post captains as far off as Cyprus and Alexandria. They knew it must be a big engagement because most of them and almost all of their archers and sailors had been summoned to England. Only those needed to service our existing contracts had been left behind.

If the past was any guide, most of the men being summoned would be keen to return to England even if it was only to rekindle old memories. It was understandable since a goodly number of them had not been back for many years.

What was certain is that there would be many requests for long shore leaves and liberties. and then there would also almost certainly be deserters when their requests were not immediately granted. That was because the men could *not* be told that their requests for shore leaves and long liberties *would* be granted when they returned from France.

Randolph and Martin were among the first to arrive with their archers and galleys. They arrived together even though they had sailed independently from Rome and from Athens's port of Piraeus. They both, they had happily reported over bowls of ale in Restormel's great hall, been absolutely astonished to see the galley of the other in the harbour when they reached

Lisbon on the same day to take on water and supplies. That is when, they both agreed, they knew that something really big was in the offing.

In the weeks that followed, the galleys of more and more of our veteran sergeant captains rowed up the Fowey with their archers and all the able-bodied recruits and rowers they could find to bring with them. Thomas Cook, Andrew Brewer, and Little Matthew all came in from Cyprus. They had all taken to heart the order to bring every available man and weapon and leave only the smallest possible force to hold their shipping posts and honour their contracts.

Then, to my great surprise and delight, Andy Ander's son sailed in with a galley and his archers and five chartered cogs full of high-quality famine-fighting grain. He had come all the way from Alexandria.

Brian, our fletcher sergeant, and Alan the smith and their seconds also came in from Cyprus. They sailed in four galleys and brought everything from their weapons works with them: tools, materials, and every fletcher and smith, including some of the refugee women fletchers, from the fletching works and smithy located along the third curtain wall of our highly fortified Cyprus post.

They had apparently fletched arrows and pounded out arrowheads all the way from Cyprus and, and as a result, landed in Cornwall with a huge and greatly appreciated supply of both longs and heavies. Brian and Alan also brought over five hundred new bladed pikes and tens of thousands of finished arrows from the dungeon of our Cyprus stronghold. And, following orders, every arrival had stopped in Lisbon and bought all the grain they could carry to help fight the famine.

The biggest surprise of all arrived two days after Thomas Cook and Matthew Little reached Cornwall—Yoram. He had come to join us after leaving Simon in charge of Cyprus with a two-year supply of food and firewood and strict instructions to always keep all the gates barred and never, under any circumstances, let anyone inside the curtain walls or surrender.

I could not believe my eyes when I saw Yoram not thirty paces away, standing on the deck of a storm-battered galley as it made its way upstream to Restormel. I was with Peter at one of our new tent camps along the Fowey as his galley slowly rowed past me. I had been talking to a four stripe sergeant captain, William Wood, about the archery training of his galley's men when I saw him. I thought I must be dreaming.

"Yoram?" *Saints above; it cannot be.* "Is that you, Yoram?" I shouted out to the arriving galley.

Yoram waved excitedly and shouted back. A few seconds later, his galley nosed into the shore, and he threw its mooring lines to the willing hands of the men lining the riverbank. He could not wait and neither could I. He jumped down into the ankle-deep shallows next to the riverbank, and I splashed out to him. We danced each other around and around in the chilly water like two frisky boys.

We splashed ashore arm in arm to the absolutely beaming smiles of several hundred archers. For some reason it seemed to greatly please the men that I was so happy and quick to recognize an old shipmate.

And I was truly pleased. My first and most important lieutenant, after my older brother of course, had set foot in the land of England for the first time in his life.

******

It was raining and quite chilly that evening, but that did not bother us at all. We built a roaring fire, lit nine candles to light Restormel's hall most brightly, and set more places for supping than the great hall had most likely ever known.

The result was a great reunion meal with eleven of the Company's original archers and more than forty sergeant captains who had subsequently made their marks and risen with us in the Company. Even Harold and George and their apprentice sergeants came up from Fowey Village to join us. As you might imagine, we stayed late into the night telling stories and greeting old friends.

My slashed face had been seen by many of those around the hastily extended table, and almost all the rest had heard about it. No one said a word about it, but a few inquired about my leg—more, I think, to commiserate or start a conversation rather than to actually hear about it.

Their concern touched me. They knew I was doing well and mostly recovered because they could see it. My beard covers the scar everywhere except alongside my eye, and my limp was just about gone except when it was damp or I was tired.

Overall, it was an absolutely splendid evening. Helen and her sisters and the cooks outdid themselves with the fresh meat and drink. Everyone got their fill and then some. We had venison soaked in wine with onions and new ale.

I sat at the head of the long table and began by announcing that Randolph and Raymond would be putting on another stripe and henceforth be lieutenant commanders, lifted a bowl to toast the king, and then we toasted our friends who had fallen and our absent friends Henry and Simon.

Then, to much laughter and cheers, I told them that when and where and how we would be raiding the Moors to free their English slaves at the request of the Pope would have to be kept a secret—because too many of us, and particularly me, were drinking too much and we could not afford to have the Moors find out and be waiting for us.

I saw Thomas and Peter nod their approval in silent understanding when I mentioned the Moors and the Pope's request. The rest of the men took it quite seriously; at least I hope so, because that was the story we wanted to get around.

It turned out to be a wonderful evening. I ended up roaring drunk and telling stories about the Company's early days after its crusade ended such as how Thomas and Yoram and I got the coins for our initial ships by killing the murderous Bishop of Damascus—and how and where we had first met Harold and Henry.

Chapter Twelve

Problems and an enemy.

Spring arrived and became a time of confusion and misunderstandings. It started when Giles, the young man from Thomas's school who had recently made his mark on the Company's list as an apprentice sergeant along with George and three others, trotted up from the Fowey Village wharf bringing me a message from retired archer Robert Rougham and his wife, our spies who managed the Red Hart tavern in Exeter.

It was and important message—the Earl of Devon had returned to Rougemont Castle on a French fishing boat. He was all by himself except for a single servant. The three nobles who had been his traveling companions and their men did not return with him.

I decided the news was worth reporting to the King and William Marshal, if only to show our good will and the sincerity of our undertaking to keep them informed. I quickly scribed several parchments reporting the earl's return.

One copy travelled by a galloper from Restormel to Launceston to Okehampton, and then Raymond's outriders carried it on to London via Windsor; the other was sent by galley to London for delivery to Windsor or wherever the King was located at the time. I was fairly sure that one or both of them would get through.

William Marshal and I had arranged for the outrider to stop at Windsor en route to see if the King or Marshal himself was in residence. If neither of them was there or nearby, the messenger was to continue on and deliver the parchment to Robert Heath, the sergeant in charge of our London shipping post. Robert would make sure it was delivered to Marshal. Marshal's messages, in turn, would be carried by a King's messenger to Okehampton for one of Raymond's outriders to deliver to me.

******

Two days later, one of the archers who had gone to France with Henry delivered a verbal message reporting Phillip's order for all French transports and fishing boats with masts to assemble in the harbour of Harfleur no later than the first day of June. Harfleur was across the bay from Honfleur where Henry's tavern was located.

The assembling of the French fleet was important news, and I promptly sent a message to William Marshal both by galloper and via a galley. In it I also repeated the first message just in case it had not arrived. It was a good thing I did, because the outrider who had carried my first message from Okehampton about the return of the Earl of Devon never arrived at Windsor and was never heard from again.

One thing is for sure, I later told Thomas when days later I finally heard about the rider's non-arrival— "from now on our messages sent overland are going to be carried every step of the way by more than one man, and each of the riders is going to be leading a fresh horse in case he was forced to run for it."

In any event, we now had a specific date, and everyone knew what it meant. Harold was quite relieved and rubbed his hands together in happy anticipation and relief when I told him the date.

Harold's relief at hearing the news was normal for fighting men in my experience. They do not like waiting once they know there is going to be a fight unless, of course, there is an advantage to be gained by waiting.

William Marshal's response to my warning message came all the way from London by a fast-moving relay of the King's gallopers. It contained its own alarming message: The King, meaning Marshal, now thinks a French army under Prince Louis will land somewhere near Exeter and join up with the rebellious English barons there.

In consequence of the French invasion, according to Sir William, the King was going to send him and part of the King's army to Ilchester to intercept and destroy the individual parties of barons traveling to Exeter to join the French. Additionally, and much worse, Sir Thomas Brereton and one hundred of the King's men were going to continue on towards Cornwall and base themselves at Okehampton in case the barons are able to get past Marshal.

I immediately sent back a message to Sir William saying the King's idea of intercepting the barons before they could assemble in Exeter was a very good one. Unfortunately, however, Okehampton could not possibly feed Brereton and his men because of the famine.

Taunton, I suggested to Sir William, was a much better location for Brereton to position his army because the severe famine in this part of England would prevent him from foraging for food. I also told him that Brereton and his men would have to bring their own food if he and his men intended to base themselves anywhere near Okehampton.

In any event, I added, Okehampton had been ordered to close its gate and keep it closed to everyone including Brereton and his men. That was because of the ladies and priests sheltering in it. We were taking no chances, I explained, of having an enemy of the king claim to be one of his supporters and gull his way in to molest them.

Of course, I said King John's idea of sending force to intercept the French was a good one. What else could I say? It would anger the King if I disagreed with him. Besides, it actually was a good idea. It was just that we want to deal with the barons ourselves and keep the King and his men out of Devon and Cornwall.

Marshal promptly replied with a message of his own, saying Brereton and his men did not need to use Taunton as their base because Peter des Roches, the archbishop of Winchester, already was holding Taunton Castle for the King and would also be trying to intercept the barons. It was too late, he said, to change the King's plan—Brereton and his men were already marching and would continue on to Okehampton after a brief pause at Ilchester to refresh themselves. *King's plan, my arse; it was Marshal's plan for sure. He is the one commanding the army.*

"You will just have to do the best you can to feed them," Marshal scribed.

Reading between the lines of Marshal's message, it sounded as though he thought des Roches was wavering as a supporter of the King and might end up standing with the rebel barons instead of against them. If that was not the case, des Roches would have welcomed Brereton's men to Taunton as reinforcements to strengthen the forces he would be using to intercept them. Alternately, of course, des Roches may have already declared for the barons and raised the drawbridge of Taunton Castle so the King's men would not be able to get in.

In any event, I quickly sent gallopers to Peter, Randolph, and Raymond with a long message explaining that the King's army was moving towards Cornwall and telling them what I wanted done—all the horse archers moved out of Okehampton so they would be available to engage in mobile operations, all available siege supplies rushed to Okehampton, and all the local people in the villages around Okehampton evacuated to Launceston and Restormel.

When Brereton arrives at Okehampton, I told my lieutenants, I want him to find no one there except for the foot archers and servants who are holding the castle and are under orders to let no one enter; and also no one in the surrounding villages from whom his men can forage.

At the same time, I sent gallopers to Raymond and my other lieutenants explaining the situation, I also ordered all but ten of Raymond's horse archers to immediately ride for Restormel with all of the castle's women and children and to also bring in with them all the people in the countryside around Okehampton who could be quickly rounded up including those that had come in for the famine food.

Raymond was also to move our horse herd and the local livestock all the way to Trematon so they could not be taken or eaten by Brereton's men. Ten of Raymond's horse archers under his lieutenant or his most dependable sergeant were to temporarily remain at Okehampton to hold it until a relief force of foot archers from Launceston arrived to relieve them. Then they too were to leave.

I also told Raymond that his horse archers were also to immediately evacuate Lady Isabel and his wife to Restormel with a strong escort, but they were not to take action against Brereton or anyone else unless he actually attacked them or made an attempt to prevent our men from entering or leaving the castle. If that happened he was to consider Brereton and his men as enemies and fight.

****** *Lieutenant Peter Sergeant.*

I used to be William's deputy, but recently I was additionally appointed to take Henry's place as the commander of all our ground forces. I was in the training camp on the Fowey when I received a copy of William's orders. It stressed the importance of quickly getting more siege supplies to Okehampton and replacing the horse archers stationed there so they could function as a mobile force. It was read to me by Giles Meadow, my sergeant apprentice from Thomas's school.

I think I understood the situation. As a result, I was in total agreement with William about sending Jeffrey and his Launceston foot archers to Okehampton and replacing them with foot archers from our camps along the Fowey.

What I understood was that William wanted to hold Okehampton for use against the French and to have Raymond's men and their horses outside its walls so they could act as the strongest possible mobile force. He was, in effect, moving our foot archers forward in order to free up the horse archers to confront the forces of the rebel barons and the French.

According to William, the possibility of King John's army trying to take Okehampton also meant we needed to quickly build up its siege supplies. The castle's reserves had been greatly depleted to feed an unexpectedly large number of food seekers coming in from throughout famine-stricken Devon to provide their labour in exchange for food.

William was certainly right about the castle's siege stores. They did indeed need to be built up so that Okehampton could withstand a long siege from anyone that tried to take it. We did not want the King or the French or anyone else to get a foothold in or near Cornwall, and certainly not on the only road between Cornwall and London.

In other words, even if it meant fighting the King's men under some guise or another, we were not going to let Brereton's men or anyone else enter or use Okehampton Castle. Similarly, we were not going to provide food for Brereton and his men that would enable them to stay anywhere near Cornwall.

When Brereton and his men reached Okehampton, we wanted them to find nothing—no people, no food, and no castle they could enter and use as a base. It would mean that people fleeing from the famine in Devon in the future would have to travel on to Launceston or Restormel if they wanted to exchange their labour for food.

****** *Peter Sergeant*

My response to receiving William's orders was to give the orders I needed to give to get the supplies moving and then gallop to Restormel in order to suggest to William that Jeffrey, the senior sergeant commanding the Launceston archers, be ordered to leave ten of the sixty-two archers now at Launceston and lead all the others on a forced march to Okehampton to replace Raymond's horse archers.

William agreed with my suggestions and sent off a galloper to Jeffrey at Launceston with the follow-up orders I had suggested and some additional instructions for him.

"If Brereton and his king's men reach Okehampton before you arrive and are waiting outside the gate, you are to march your men right past them and go in through Okehampton's gate without stopping to parley with Brereton and his men for any reason. You are to walk right through his lines and enter the castle even if it means you have to fight to get through them."

Even if Brereton and his men arrive before Jeffrey and his men, I doubt they would know enough about our intentions to do any more than watch as Jeffrey marched his men right past them and into the castle. I thought it unlikely Brereton would immediately start fighting with some of the king's supporters. Indeed, I was counting on it when I made my suggestion.

After I reached Restormel and spoke with William, and with his approval, I immediately led fifty of Restormel's archers on a forced march to Launceston to further reinforce it by replacing some of the men who were on their way to reinforce Okehampton. I put them in horse carts with two-horse teams and told the drivers to take them as fast and far as their horses could go.

When the horses were finished, the men were to dismount and march non-stop at their highest possible speed until they reached Launceston. William was right; we were in a race against time.

When this is over we need to think about establishing a strong force of Raymond's horse archers here at Restormel; we need a mobile force in this part of Cornwall in addition to having one across the river at Okehampton. The number of horses at our horse farm is

growing, so we should soon be able to mount at least
some of the additional men.

****** *Peter Sergeant*

A few hours later Captain William and I were standing on the muddy riverbank next to the floating wharf on the Fowey watching the archers I would lead to Launceston form up. That was when Harold and his new sergeant apprentice and scribe, William's son George, arrived on foot. They had been on a supply-carrying cog being towed up the river by one of our galleys. They walked over to join us just as it started to rain.

Harold and George were aboard the cog because I had sent a galloper to Fowey Village explaining the need for fast action and asking Harold to drop everything and get the all the available supplies up the river as soon as possible. He and George were on the first cog to make sure it got safely up the river with the famine supplies it was carrying; William was similarly waiting at the river wharf next to our camp to make sure the cog's cargo of food supplies was quickly loaded on the waiting horse wagons and they were immediately sent off to Okehampton.

Everyone was in a hurry and rightly so. We needed to get the food supplies from the cog to Okehampton Castle, move the local population out of harm's way, and raise the castle's drawbridge before Sir Thomas Brereton and his force of knights and soldiers arrived to "help" us fight the barons and the French.

We would almost certainly be able to get Raymond's men and the women out of the castle and the archers from Launceston inside to replace them, even if it meant a fight, but I was not at all sure the food supplies would reach Okehampton before Brereton arrived. It was going to be difficult, but we would have to try. Okehampton's food reserves had been depleted by the famine. Without more food, anyone who attacked Okehampton was likely to take it by starving out its defenders.

****** *William*

I was standing on the riverbank with Peter and Harold and their apprentice sergeants because I could not stay away; I wanted to see how they were responding to the order I had sent them. What I saw as I dismounted my horse and joined them was reassuring—a long line of horse-drawn wains was being rapidly loaded all along the cart path that runs along the river past the camp's floating wharf.

It was a sight to see—bustling and shouting archers and sailors had formed a line and were passing the sacks of food and weapons from man to man, all the way from the newly arrived supply cog and across the bobbing wharf and on to the line of men who were loading the wains and carts.

Everything appeared chaotic, but if you looked closely you could see it was highly organized.

"Where is the sergeant in charge of the supply train?" shouted Peter as I stepped back to avoid being knocked aside by a sailor carrying a great armful of bladed pikes. They were being loaded in the wagons for the archers to use if the wagons were attacked.

A grimacing, white-faced, three stripe sergeant hurried up to report to Peter and knuckled his forehead to salute. Sweat was pouring off him, and he was holding his right side. It was instantly apparent that he was in a great deal of pain.

"My God, Anthony. What happened to you? Are you all right?" Peter asked.

"I am fine, Peter. Just a little twitch in my side, that is all. It started yesterday and has not let up ever since. I will get through it."

"Little twitch, my arse. You have got a big hurt, and I can see you do."

Damn! If Anthony's hurt is where he is touching with his right hand, he is probably either got a rip from lifting something heavy or one of those really painful inside hurts that can kill a man.

****** *William*

I watched as Peter sent off the agonized sergeant to see if the camp's barber could do anything for him. Then things went from bad to worse; there were no senior sergeants immediately available to take his place. They had all gone with their companies to the training camps we had set up around Fowey Village. Worse, the men left behind to labour on the wharf and drive the wains and horse carts were new archers that had recently been apprentice archers. Only a handful of the older, chosen men had been left to sergeant them.

"Those wagons have got to go this minute, even if I have to ride with them and sergeant them myself," I said to Peter and Harold. "We are running out of time."

"I will take them, Father," my son George volunteered. Peter, Harold, and I turned and looked at George in surprise. "I am rested and ready to go, and I know how to deliver supplies."

Harold turned and looked at me and then shrugged his agreement; so did Peter.

Chapter Thirteen

My second command and the King's men arrive.

My father stared at me thoughtfully for what seemed like a long time. Finally, he nodded and said, "Well, he is young and green and the only sergeant we have available under the circumstances. And he has read the parchments and heard us talking, so at least he knows what needs to be done and why. So yes, you can go."

I ran to the front of the column and slapped the nearside horse in the rump to get it moving forward on the muddy cart path. When I got past the wain at the front of the line, I stood there pumping my arm to encourage the drivers to move faster. After the last wain came past, I ran back and sheepishly asked my father if I could borrow his horse.

****** *George son of William*

Our wains and carts moved right along all afternoon and into the night under the moonlight. Refugees coming the other way moved off the path to let us past. We continued all that night and all next day and all the next night. We never stopped except for a few hours yesterday and then again last night to rest the horses.

There were two men on each wain so they could take turns driving the two-horse teams. We made good time because we drove the horses hard with only the briefest of stops for grain and water.

Periodically, the column stopped when wheels broke or the wains got stuck for some reason or another. But the column never stopped for long—we either quickly fixed the problem or we pulled the broken wain aside and a swarm of archers off-loaded its supplies on to the empty wains traveling at the end of the column.

We started with five empty wains, and four of them were in use by noon of the third day when we reached Launceston ford and began to move across the River Tamar and into Devon. The wains they replaced were left empty and abandoned along the side of the road. We will come back and fetch them on our way back home.

Everything changed a few miles before we reached the Launceston ford when we met the first of several outriders coming west on the road from Okehampton. From them we learnt Raymond and the women from the castle and the horse archers and local villagers were now safely across the Tamar and have almost certainly reached Launceston. They would rest there and then go on to Restormel as soon as our convoy passes and the road is clear.

The outriders also told us a large force of knights led by a King's man by the name of Sir Thomas Brereton had reached Okehampton and was camped in front of the castle's raised drawbridge—and was desperately in need of food. We would be arriving too late to resupply Okehampton. It meant we would have to divert to Launceston.

A few minutes later, our own outrider galloped in to report a large force of men coming towards us on the cart path from Launceston. It was Raymond and his horse archers, more than a hundred of them. They were coming to give us the same warning about possible trouble ahead with Brereton and to escort us to Launceston or back to Restormel.

Raymond's force turned out to be every hors earcher he had available. The rest of his men were busy moving the local livestock and the mares and stallions of our horse farm further west beyond Trematon.

Even though I knew the approaching riders were almost certainly Raymond and our horse archers, I dismounted my men and had them quickly hobble the cart horses and form up seven men deep in the battle formation we use to fight mounted knights and their men-at-arms. It was good practice for us and out here one never knows for sure.

"Hello, Uncle Raymond. It was good to see you again."

All of the surviving original archers are my uncles and have been since they helped my father and Uncle Thomas carry me over the wall of Lord Edmund's castle and bring me to England along with the coins and galleys they picked up along the way.

"Hello yourself, young George. How are you, lad? I got the parchment about a wagon train of siege supplies being on its way to Okehampton, but I did not know you would be leading them.

"We have come to escort you to Launceston. There is trouble ahead. The damn King sent an army to stop the barons from reaching Rougemont. He does not trust us to do the job, does he? He is a damn fool, that is what he is. He sent them into a famine without food."

I got the wains moving again, and then Uncle Raymond and I talked as we rode together. We had not seen much of each other in recent years, and we had not had a chance to talk at all at my father's big dinner at Restormel.

Raymond told me the archers from Launceston arrived in time for all his men to leave before the King's men appeared. He also said almost all the Okehampton villagers and those that had come there to labour for famine food had walked to Launceston so they could keep eating. "We used a couple of the village hay wains to carry those who were not strong enough to walk."

That the local people and those who came in to work for famine food were no longer at Okehampton was important; yes, it was. It meant that twenty of the wains in my convoy, those with famine food that destined for the villages and for the people who had come in because of the famine, could now go to Launceston because that was where the people would now be waiting.

The problem was that thirty-eight wains were supposed to go to Okehampton carrying the grain and dried fish for the castle's siege reserves. That would have been enough for a garrison of fifty archers to hold out for more than a year, and may even longer if they ate the horses and tightened their belts.

Now, unless we could get them past the King's men and into Okehampton, the food would be going to Launceston and Okehampton would not be able to hold out for very long. At least that is what we thought at the time.

******

We moved the wains and carts over the Tamar ford above Launceston behind a great screen of Raymond's horse archers without even slowing down. I was at the ford watching the last three wains lurch and splash their way across the river to join the column waiting on the other side of the river when I saw the horse archers screen coming back fast and quickly dismount into defensive positions at the head of the column.

Almost immediately, their horse holders began galloping their horses back across the ford to the Launceston side of the river. It did not look like a practice to me, and from the looks on the men's faces as they galloped past us with the horses, they did not think it was either.

My response was to put my horse into a great splashing gallop across the ford, shouting for my men to make a half turn and place the heavily loaded wains and carts so close together that their beds touched. Then they were to dismoun, hobble and blindfold their horses so they would not run, and form up in battle formation on the left side of the road.

The beds of the wagons and wains were soon side by side and so close together that a horse could not ride between them. And they were facing with their sterns all pointed in the same direction to block off any knights and riders that tried to roll up our line of fighting men by charging at us from our right. The river was immediately behind us such that the last two wains and their horses were actually parked in the water.

All in all it was a fairly strong position with the carts blocking off a charge from our right and the river behind us. It was what Raymond told me I was to do if it looked like there might be a fight. He would, he said, position his men on the other side of the path so that the line of carts would protect his lines from being rolled up by a knightly charge coming from the left.

Between us, we had almost two hundred heavily armed archers. Unfortunately, my seventy-six on the left side of the cart path were mostly newly promoted archers that were apprentices until a few weeks ago. Good men all, but green as grass like me.

I stayed on my horse and called out my orders as the archers jumped down from the wains, grabbed their bows and pikes, and formed up in the seven men deep fighting formation the Company uses against knights on horseback. They quickly began laying out their weapons.

My men were side by side in an eleven-man front. I did not divide them and position some of them in the rear of the column because there would be no place for them to stand except in the water.

Uncle Raymond came trotting up on his splendid black Arabian gelding as my men finished getting into position. He was sitting erect and alert, every inch a battle captain.

"There is a big force of riders coming this way on the Okehampton road, Sergeant," he said to me quite formally. "There are at least a hundred of them, maybe more. My outriders say they look like knights and their men-at-arms. It is almost certainly Brereton and his men. Come with me."

We rode side by side until we got out in front a good ways past the hastily placed range markers of our strongest archers. Then we stopped on the cart path and waited. A few minutes later, one of Raymond's outriders, a chosen man wearing two stripes, came pounding down the road on a lathered horse and pulled up to report.

"There be knights on the road ahead of us, captain, and they be coming this way. I counted about a hundred of the bastards all together. Maybe half are knights wearing armour, and they have all got helmets and either hauberks or cuirasses. I am not sure they know we are here. They were riding real easy and have their helmets off."

"Good man, Ralphie. Stay here with us and let your horse cool down and rest a bit. This here is Sergeant George. We came out of Syria together in rags years ago, and we have been together in the Company ever since." Then he added with a smile, "We were both a lot younger then, eh George?"

Ralphie and I smiled at each other and lifted our hands to acknowledge the introduction. What I saw was a slender man with a full, brown beard and two stripes on the Egyptian gown he wore under his hooded winter cloak. A veteran for sure.

"Ahh. Yes, here they come," Raymond said to no one in particular.

In the distance we could see movement through the leafless trees to our right front. They were on the road and riding towards us, but not in a battle formation.

* * * * * *

About five minutes later the first of the riders came around the curve in the path and into full view. When the leaders saw us, they pulled up their horses and looked at us. After a short wait, they put on their helmets and began slowly and cautiously walking their horses towards us as more and more riders came into view behind them.

Ralphie had been right; there were at least one hundred of them. From the looks of them and how they rode, they were almost all knights and their squires and sergeants, fighting men for sure. From this distance I could not tell for sure, but it did not seem to me that any of them were carrying bows.

Raymond raised his open hand in greeting, put a big smile on his face, and slowly walked his horse towards them.

"Come with me," Raymond ordered. "Smile and act friendly, but be prepared to turn and run for it."

We walked our horses forward, and so did the men coming towards us. My father's horse was the finest horse I had ever ridden.

The distance between us closed rapidly and they kept coming. When we got to within about two hundred paces, Raymond turned his horse around, and we headed back in the other direction towards our men in order to maintain the distance between us and the approaching army. I was anxious and kept looking back over my shoulder.

"Always keep enough distance so you can get away clean without getting hit by a short push from your own men," Raymond muttered to me. I started to unsling my bow, but Raymond hissed at me to stop. "Act friendly, damn it."

Turning around and walking our horses to maintain a safe distance from the oncoming riders had the desired effect. One of the men at the front of the horsemen raised his hand and the main body of riders behind him halted.

He and two other riders rode forward towards the three of us. All were helmeted knights with their visors up, and all three of them had some form of a bear's head painted on their shields. Their swords were not drawn, and none of the three were carrying bows. The leader's hand was raised in a somewhat dismissive and insolent gesture of peaceful greeting as they trotted up to us.

At least it struck me as being dismissive and insolent, as Ralphie and I followed Raymond's lead and turned our horses back to face them as a friendly group of men would do.

"Who are you and why are you here?" Raymond asked in a deep, strong voice before anyone else could speak.

"I am Sir Thomas Brereton and we are King's men. Who are you?"

"We are men of the Earl of Cornwall's Company of Archers, and this is our road between the Company's keeps at Launceston and Okehampton. Are you traveling in peace? Do you need someone to guide you?"

"What we need is food. Do you have any?"

"We have barely enough for ourselves. There is a famine fallen on the land, as I am sure you know,"

Raymond replied with a sad smile and a pleasant sound to his voice.

"What have you in the wains?" was the knight's response. He asked with a tone of arrogant demand in his voice as he made a gesture of his hand towards the line of wains behind the archers.

"Supplies for Okehampton," Raymond replied.

Uncle Raymond was trying not to provoke them. I probably would have said, "That is no concern of yours," and been rather arrogant about it. On the other hand, Raymond was an experienced negotiator and I was not. It was very interesting; I was fascinated and being learnt all at the same time.

"We will see about that," the knight said. He gestured for the man on his right to ride forward and look.

"Hold!" Raymond raised his hand in a signal for the rider to stop. "Those men down there in front of the wains are archers, and they are under orders to push arrows into anyone who comes within their range. There is no need for your man to die for nothing, is there?"

Raymond continued after a brief pause.

"Well then, Sir Knight, you say you and your men are supporters of the King; well, so is the Earl of Cornwall. The King would not be pleased if his supporters fight each other instead of the French and the rebel barons, would he?"

Sir Thomas's reply was more than a little curt and arrogant.

"He would want you to feed your betters; that is what would please the King. We are taking the food in those wains."

And with that, the knight wheeled his horse around and began to ride back to his men.

"Wait," said Raymond. "There is no need for us to fight, Sir Thomas. Let us all be reasonable and try to find a solution. These are hard times for everyone."

The knight wheeled his horse around and came back a few steps to listen.

"I will tell you what, Sir Thomas," Raymond offered. "If you send your men forward one at a time, we will give each of them enough grain and dried fish to get them back to Ilchester where William Marshal is reported to be camped. He has received a shipment of food I am told."

"No. I will tell *you* what, you insolent cur. I will give your men two minutes to get their personal belongings out of the wains and be gone. Then I am going to take the wagons and what is in them for the King's army."

******

Raymond started to say something, but then he shrugged, kicked his horse in the ribs, and led us back to our men at a canter.

"Well, no one can say I did not try," he shouted over his shoulder to me as we trotted back to our men.

"Give your reins to Ralphie," Raymond ordered me as he dismounted and shouted, "Skinny Bill, get over here. I have got a job for you and your lads."

Then he turned to Ralphie.

"Ralphie, get you back to the horse holders and tell them to bring the riding horses of Bill and his men back across the ford. Only the riding horses of Bill and his men, mind you, not his supply horses. Tell John to have the other horse holders stay where they are and stand firm."

Ralphie knuckled his forehead in a salute and galloped off leading our horses. Less than a minute later, an extremely plump and very short, beardless archer without a hair on his head came jogging up with an expectant look on his face and short of breath. He had the three stripes of a sergeant on his tunic and one of the reddest faces I have ever seen. Skinny he was not, but somehow the nickname seemed to fit him.

"Bill, they would be bringing up your men's riding horses in a couple of minutes. It looks like there is going to be a fight. Mount your men and take them through the trees over there and get around behind that lot. Bring all your extra arrows with you."

Raymond pointed to where he wanted Bill to take his men and then added his fighting orders.

"Bill, I want you and your men to stay mounted. Do not start anything, but if they attack us, I want you to hit them in their rear and stay tight against them using your bows until they break. Take prisoners if you can, but do not let any of them get away.

"You know the drill. No matter what happens, do not push on them until the fighting starts down here. You are not to start it; hopefully, they will come to their senses and withdraw without a fight. If they do withdraw you are to pull back and let them go in peace.

"And you, Sergeant George, you go see to your men. Make sure they have got their arrows unwrapped and their range markers out to the front and to your left. And make sure they have water, mind you, and proper holes to set their pikes."

Chapter Fourteen

My first real battle command.

We laid out our arrow bales, put out the range markers and water skins, and waited. I had seventy-six men from my wains plus me. As I walked up and down, getting them into position and checking each man's readiness, I realized there was not a sergeant among them. They were almost all new archers that had just gotten their first stripe. Most of them were like me— they had never been in a real battle.

Until today, the closest I have ever been to a real battle was when I was in the rear with Uncle Thomas when Lord Courtenay came out of Okehampton to attack us when we were traveling to London. That is when His Lordship got himself and his friends killed and we somehow ended up with Okehampton for our trouble.

My men were not what I expected. Instead of the veteran sergeants my fellow students and I had been told would be there to support us and repeat our commands, there were only five two-stripe chosen men that had been left among the new archers to supervise their work as wagon and wain drivers.

I understood that I would have to make do with what I had. So I quickly moved the chosen men around so each would be an acting sergeant in the key fourth-line position where the file sergeants and the commander stand during a battle.

When I finished, my little company was standing in somewhat of a square that was eleven men across and seven men deep. More specifically, the first three of each front-to-back line of seven men were archers with pikes, then there was a gap of ten paces, and then four more archers without pikes. In a regular company of foot archers, the fourth man would be the sergeant of the seven men and a veteran of many battles.

"Be ready to push, lads," I shouted out as I walked through the ranks one of my little band one last time to make sure every man was in place and ready. "Be ready to push longs and to change to heavies when you hear the command."

Yes, I said push. According to my uncle Thomas, regular archers such as those the king's of England and France hold their bows out in front of them and pull back on their bowstrings to launch their arrows. Longbow men are different. We hold our bowstrings and push out our bows with a great thrust to launch our arrows. That push and our much longer and stronger bows is why only strong men can push out a longbow. It is also why our longs fly so much further and our heavies with their additional weight and iron heads can penetrate armour. At least that is what Uncle Thomas always told us in our school. I hope it is true.

I had barely finished getting my chosen men in place and loudly reminding them, and everyone else, of their duties as the fourth man and commander of the file when warning cries of "here they come" erupted. The men were supposed to stay silent so the sergeants' commands could be heard, but my men were green and nervous, and there began to be a lot of talking in the ranks.

Everyone is nervous, particularly me. Actually, I am not nervous; I am excited. I have never done this before—command men in a real battle, I mean. I like it.

"Silence in the ranks!" I roared as I slipped through the front three lines to stand as a sergeant captain in front of my men for the first time in my life. Then I gave the first real battle order I had ever given.

"Prepare to nock longs. Nock your longs. Wait for my order to pick your man and push." It was the first of our basic fighting commands, and every man had heard it a thousand times whilst training as an apprentice archer.

Truth be told, I was so bewitched watching the mounted men moving towards us that I probably would have forgotten to give the order if I had not heard Raymond and his sergeants bellowing it out from their positions in front of the squares to my right.

I waited in front of my men with my longbow in my hand and watched in absolute fascination as the mounted men walked their horses past our hastily paced off range markers and into our kill zone. It was as if they did not know how far our longs could fly. *We should have brought stakes and caltrops. Why are we not pushing?*

We did not launch our longs even though we could have reached the men forming up to charge us. Instead, we watched and waited, as Raymond had told me we must, until he and he alone gave the command to launch. The knights and their men slowly walked their horses towards us and began to spread out on both sides of the cart road to the extent they could for all the trees and the ditch running along either side of it.

It was almost as if they expected us to break and run from the sight of them, as a gathering of rebellious peasants might run when the knights arrive to disperse them. It was silent in our ranks and in the bare trees of the forest along the road—so silent we could hear the hoofs of the knights' horses hitting the ground and snatches of their talking.

As I watched the knights in front of us, I heard their shouts and orders increase as they organized themselves and got ready to put their spurs to their horses and begin their charge. They were still getting themselves organized when we heard the shouted order we had all been expecting from Raymond. I loudly repeated it and so did the chosen men acting in the sergeants' positions in the fourth rank of each seven-man file.

"Pick your man and get ready to push with longs."

It was the traditional signal for longbow men to hold tight to their bowstrings and get ready to push out their bows to launch their arrows. It was also to let them know I would now be stepping back to the fourth line and be ready to push arrows out my own longbow.

A moment later, Raymond gave the order sending us to war, and we all shouted it as well.

"Push longs and continue! Push longs and continue!"

All around me I heard the grunts and cries as the archers pushed their bows out from their bodies to launch their lighter long-distance arrows towards the knights who were slowly moving towards and getting ready to charge.

Once the shooting began, I continued to push out arrows and constantly shouted the command "push longs" as a battle commander is expected to do; the newly appointed sergeants, veterans all, repeated them as sergeants are expected to do. All around me I could hear the shouts to "push," the grunts of the archers as they did so, and the distinctive cracking sound of their bowstrings as they hit against the archers' leather wrist protectors.

"Pick your man and push longs; pick your man and push longs."

My men's rapid pushing out of arrows would continue until I gave a new command for my acting file sergeants to repeat. I knew them all by heart—the various commands, that is. I certainly should; I had repeated them almost every day since Uncle Thomas gave me my first bow and began teaching us boys to be sergeants.

******

A virtual hailstorm of arrows began dropping on the slowly moving and still milling about mass of knights and their horses and men. It instantly caused much panic and movement among them as men were hit and wounded horses bolted and threw their riders.

Seconds later, some of the knights put spurs to their horses and charged toward us. Most of the others, at least those still on their horses, soon followed behind them as if they were a herd of sheep.

Within seconds, a disorganized mob of armour-wearing men on horses bore down on us. Many of them were carrying lances. It was as if they thought that fighting archers and pike men would be the same as being in a tournament or joust.

The knights and their men responded to the hail of arrows, as you might imagine, by quickly dropping their visors. In that instant they reduced their chance of taking an arrow in the face but became virtually blind just as they began their charge and their horses picked up speed.

Horses and men went down even before the charge began and continued to fall or turn off to the side and go down as the surviving knights pounded down the cart path towards us through a constant hail of arrows. My shouted orders changed as the gap between the charging knights and my little band of men rapidly narrowed.

"Ready pikes and be ready to ground your pikes. Now ground your pikes. Ground your pikes. Heavies. Use your heavies."

As the surviving horsemen thundered down on us, the archers in our first three ranks put down their bows and placed the butt of their pikes in the little hole each had dug in the ground. Then each kneeled—and held his pike with both hands to aim its point at the chest of the horse of whatever knight was coming straight at him.

Only forty or so, and perhaps fewer, of the charging riders reached our front line. And most of those who did never even saw our long and bladed pikes come up or realized what they meant. Those few who did, tried to turn their horses; several in the rear succeeded, only to take multiple arrows in their backs. Most did not. They ran their horses straight onto our pikes and impaled them.

Raymond's men in the centre and on our right took most of the knights that reached our lines. Only six or seven charged on to our pikes of my men on the left and, in so-doing, killed their horses and themselves. It was not so much that the pikes took the knights. They did not; they mostly took the horses the knights were riding.

All along our line there were the screams of horses and the sharp *crack* as some of the heavy oak poles of the pikes shattered under the weight of the charging horses. The horses were stopped in their tracks and typically fell off to one side or the other. Their riders, on the other hand, were still a danger because most of them flew off their suddenly stopped horses and kept coming until they crashed to the ground or fell on top of the men in our first three lines or into the ten paces of open ground behind in front of our third and fourth lines of archers.

As soon as the last charging knight in front of us was unhorsed, the acting sergeants in the fourth line and I moved forward with our knives to finish off any of our attackers that were still alive—as many of the horsemen still were despite their broken bones.

One of the unhorsed knights had come down on top of the pike-holding archers in front of me. He was not moving, but I stepped forward and slipped my dagger under his helmet and into his throat to make sure.

To kill unhorsed knights was why our fourth line was ten paces behind the third. The knights rarely got to the fourth line when they came flying off their piked horses. Leaving the open space where they could land was something Uncle Thomas said the Company had learnt years ago on Cyprus when it fought Cyprus's king over some men of ours he had taken for ransom. I had been quite young at the time and did not remember much about Cyprus at all.

It had been quite noisy in our ranks, what with all the shouts and cries and the screaming horses and men. It seemed to go on forever. Suddenly, everything was quiet all around me. Only then did I hear Raymond bellowing at me to get off my arse and get my sergeants out to finish off the knights and horses stretched out on the ground in front of us.

I should have acted faster. Knights and their horses were all over the ground in front of us and around us. Some of the knights lay unmoving, but I could see others struggling to get to their feet and a few that had succeeded and were trying to walk away.

They did not get far.

Chapter Fifteen

The aftermath.

"That is a nice collection. We will fetch some decent coins when we sell them," Raymond said as he and Rollie and I stood looking at the growing pile of armour and weapons being gathered from the fallen knights and their retainers.

"But it cost us a high price," Raymond said. "Two of my men were killed, and I have got at least six with broken bones and such, including one of my best sergeants who took a lance and might be needing a mercy."

Also in our booty were more than two dozen good horses, if you included the horses whose cuts and slashes could be healed sufficient to be added to our herd or, more likely, sold because they were bred big to carry armoured knights rather than fast moving horse archers.

We also took enough clothes and tents and saddles and such to overfill an entire wain. There were eight prisoners of which not a one was a knight, probably because, as everyone knows, knights tend to be too arrogant and unwilling to behave themselves when they are captured.

I myself did not see any prisoners being taken on the battlefield. They must have been captured by the riders Raymond sent around to cut off the escapers and round up the knights' handful of servants.

We stayed on the battlefield that night to bury the dead and barber our wounded, even though it was hard to understand why taking more blood from a wounded man would help him recover or how it would set his broken bones. I resolved to ask my uncle Thomas more about barbering. He knows about such things, being as he has talked to several Greek physicians and has read books and such.

I slept under a wain that evening, as we always do in case of rain, though it proved to be unnecessary. The next morning, we put our wounded on top of the supplies in the wains and travelled on the cart road to Okehampton. One of our wounded cried out when the wain rattled about on the rutted road. He thanked us profusely when we gave him more flower paste to eat. Raymond's dangerously ill sergeant had an ashen face but was still with us when we reached Okehampton in time for our evening food.

The castle's garrison of foot archers from Launceston was more than a little pleased to see us and to be reinforced and resupplied. They were elated when they heard the knights and soldiers that had been camping outside the gate would not be returning. They said they knew something good had happened when they watched Raymond's outriders gallop into what was left of the knights' old camp and begin looking for loot.

To celebrate our victory and the horse archers' return to their base at Okehampton, we cooked flatbread that evening and cut strips off some of the sheep from the flock kept inside the walls and toasted them over campfires in the bailey. In addition, every man was given several bowls of ale from the garrison's two ale barrels and an onion from those few remaining in the castle's dungeon. We also fed three village families with young children that had somehow been left behind in the evacuation or, perhaps, were overlooked or newly arrived.

Rollie and I traded our onions to Raymond's cook for a rack of mutton and some pinches of salt. Sam Cook is famous among the archers for being the Company's best cook. Some say he is even better than Thomas Cook when the lieutenants and senior sergeants are not around to hear them and disagree.

Okehampton Castle was full to overflowing with men. My men and our three wounded slept in the great hall and the Launceston archers continued sleeping in the wall towers where they had been camped ever since they first arrived. The horse archers slept in their own beds in the stalls that were their barracks along the curtain wall next to the stables. The only thing they were missing were their families who had been evacuated to Restormel.

Raymond took his own room and graciously offered his sergeant apprentice and me the use of the other upstairs room and the bed that had been hurriedly vacated by Lady Isabel and her maidservant when they left for Launceston.

My men slept downstairs in the great hall with a roaring fire to keep them warm. I made sure our wounded men got the best places as Uncle Thomas had taught us in our school. The prisoners got tossed into the dungeon cell where the onions had been stored. There were some onions left so they were able to have something to eat.

I wonder what Lady Isabel would say about Raymond offering Rollie and me the use of her room and bed. Are she and her maid not coming back? Raymond said it was to keep us close in case he needed us to read or scribe, but I wonder.

Raymond's apprentice sergeant was Rollie, a long-time friend and fellow student ever since Cyprus. Rollie and I stayed up half the night talking about what had happened and who had done what.

We were both still excited about our first battle and could hardly sleep, what with telling each other all about what we had seen and heard and done. Rollie was almost hit by a knight when his horse was stopped by a pike and his rider kept going. The knight broke his neck but could still speak until one of Raymond's archers gave him a mercy. Rollie could not stop talking about him.

******

On our fifth morning at Okehampton, just as we were preparing to leave, a messenger came in with a long parchment for Raymond from my father. I was there when Rollie read it to him.

The message said Sir William Marshal was on his way to Okehampton from his camp in Ilchester to inquire about what happened to Brereton and his men. As a result, someone that was at the battle had to stay and tell Sir William all about it and then hurry to Restormel to report his response. That someone was me.

There was also a separate parchment for me with specific orders as to what I was to say to Sir William and what I was not to say. Uncle Raymond left two of his outriders with me and a spare riding horse for each of us. We were to leave for Restormel as soon as I finished speaking with Sir William.

Not everyone was ordered to leave. The Launceston archers were to stay and temporarily garrison Okehampton until the horse archers returned. Everyone else, including any prisoners, were ordered to leave immediately for Restormel.

The Launceston men were given specific orders to remain inside Okehampton's walls with the drawbridge up and on high alert at all times. No one, not even Sir William and his men, was to be allowed into the castle for any reason "because there are noble ladies and priests inside to whom we have sworn no one would be allowed to enter." *Actually, there had been only one noble lady at Okehampton and she was long gone to Restormel. I was sure of that; I had been using her bed for the past five days.*

****** *George*

Sir William Marshal arrived at Okehampton late in the morning with about forty men. They appeared to be his household knights. I was standing by my horse outside the castle wall with my two outriders when they trotted up. I was wearing a priest's robe and carrying no weapons except a wooden cross and my hidden wrist knives.

Sir William reined in his horse in front of me and dismounted with a weary groan. The drawbridge was up, and the Restormel archers and our wounded men were in the castle with its gate closed. The archers were standing on the battlements so they could be seen. Everyone else was on their way to Restormel in response to my father's summons.

We were hopeful Sir William and our enemies, whoever they might turn out to be, would not ever know how few men we actually have defending the castle. If they did know, they might be misled by the small number of defenders and try to take it. And then they would most likely die as the men in the castle were well-trained, well-equipped, and well-captained archers—and there were more than enough of them to hold it for quite some time.

Having never done anything like this before, I was more than a little anxious when the leader of the riders dismounted. But I knuckled my head, bowed to him, and followed my orders.

I immediately explained I was a priest who been at the battle with Brereton at the Launceston ford. I had, I said, received a parchment from my bishop ordering me not to return to Restormel "until I describe to Sir William Marshal exactly what happened when the robbers attacked the Bishop's wains." What I was ordered not tell him was that I was my father's son or that I had been told what to say and what not to say. *Robbers? Yes, robbers, I was told to always use the word* robbers *when describing the battle.*

Sir William identified himself and asked some pointed questions. He seemed surprised when I told him I had been in charge of the men driving wains filled with famine food, and we had been assisted in fighting off the robbers by some hundred or so of the Earl of Cornwall's seagoing men.

The Earl of Cornwall's men were only sailors, I explained, and were accompanying us at the Bishop's request, because there had been reports of a band of robbers on the road. We were, I explained to Sir William, using the wains to bring famine food to the people living in Okehampton and in the villages around it.

"The Bishop sold some of the church plates and relics to get enough coins to buy the food," I confided to him as I had been ordered to do. "He is a good man and wanted to make sure it was delivered. That is why all the people love him."

It was quickly apparent that all Sir William knew about the battle was what had been scribed on the parchment my father sent him.

In response to Sir William's questions I described how the Earl's lieutenant had tried to reason with the robbers and even offered them food if they would go away in peace. Then I used a stick and scratched on the dirt to describe how the robbers charged down the cart path against us.

"It was terrible, Sir William, just terrible. Several of the Earl of Cornwall's best seagoing men were killed and others wounded when the spears they braced into the ground stopped the robbers' horses in their tracks. The robbers came flying off their horses and landed amongst them.

"It was the arrows what did for the robbers. Two of the Earl's men had bows and began shooting arrows when the robbers charged down the road towards us. So the robbers pulled down their visors and let their horses which were wearing blinders continue charging down the road at us—until they ran themselves straight onto the long spears the sailors were carrying.

"The Bishop thinks it was God's Will that anyone that attacks or works against the Earl and his men soon dies or comes down with a terrible pox,"

I spoke so the men standing nearby could hear.

"He says God protects them because they keep their word and are always willing to fight to free Englishmen that are being held as slaves."

I did not understand why my father told me to be sure to confide this to Sir William loudly enough so others could hear; I hope he will explain it to me later.

Sir William nodded. "How do you know Sir Thomas was among the robbers?"

Good! Now I have got him thinking of Brereton and his men as robbers just as Father wanted me to do.

"The Earl's men took several of the robber's servants as prisoners, Sir William. One of them identified Sir Thomas as their captain."

"The King will not like this, not one bit. He will give Brereton and his men a good going over, I am sure; and so will I when I find them."

"Well . . . uh . . . Sir William, that might be difficult," I said and explained—the difficulty being that Sir Thomas and almost all of his knights were dead as a result of blindly running themselves on to the spears of the Church's relief convoy in an effort to steal its supplies.

We spoke a bit more, and I scraped the ground with a stick once again to show where the drivers and the Earl's seafaring men had stood, how the robbers attacked, and where the robbers' bodies had been left as a caution to others. "And of course I prayed over their bodies before we rode on."

Two hours later, a stunned and almost speechless Sir William was on his way back to Ilchester, and my two escorts and I were pounding down the cart path on our way to Restormel to report his desparture.

Chapter Sixteen

Getting ready for war.

Our archers and sailors continued to train and practice as the weather got warmer as spring arrived. Everything remained relatively quiet for several weeks. It was a fine time indeed. My women were pleased to be with me, and I took George and the boys hunting on several occasions. We had a fine time and brought in many hart and wild boar for the men to eat.

Then two different gallopers came into camp less than an hour apart. Their messages changed everything. The first, a King's messenger, brought me a parchment from William Marshal. Sir William reported he had had a sad but satisfactory visit to Okehampton in the spring to learn more about the tragedy that had befallen the late and apparently somewhat lamented Sir Thomas Brereton.

"It appears," Marshal scribed, "that Sir Thomas mistook a train of church wains your sailors were defending to be French invaders and attacked them in the belief he was fighting for his King. His family and friends will miss him."

Such ox shite. Marshal knows damn well what happened to Brereton, but it was fine with me if he wants to pretend the damn fool died fighting for the King. He is probably trying to save Brereton's fief in Chester for his son.

What now concerned him, Marshal scribed, was information he had just received from the King suggesting my men and I would soon be sailing to free slaves from the Moors at the request of the Pope. He wanted to know if it meant we no longer intended to help the King intercept the barons that were now thought to be bypassing Ilchester and assembling their forces around Exeter.

I immediately dispatched a reply. I lied a little, but mostly I told the truth. I assured Sir William the report the King received was not accurate. My men, I scribed, were committed to fighting the French and their allies. I swore it as an oath. I also swore we had no plans to sail against the Moors until the threat of a French invasion was finished. *But now at least we know King John has a spy somewhere in our camp.*

What I had scribed and sent to Sir William about our preparing to fight the French was true. What I did not tell him was that we had no intention of helping the King fight the barons except in Devon and Cornwall.

I also did not tell Sir William that my mentioning the Moors and the freeing of their slaves was a ploy to gull the French king into thinking he could safely assemble his invasion transports without simultaneously boarding his army to protect them.

The second messenger brought much more important news. Henry and his men had been fishing off Harfleur every day for the past fortnight and spent time in the Harfleur taverns each evening after they sold their catch. They reported that the gathering and supplying of the French fleet in and around Harfleur looked as if it would be completed in less than a fortnight. The French soldiers and mercenaries mustering south of Paris were expected to begin their march to Harfleur in the coming week.

It was time, Henry suggested, for him to return to his tavern and his wife and for us to sail for France. And then, Henry being Henry, he had his messenger tell me we had all made the right choices when we decided to be archers, pirate-takers, and tavern keepers; it was a lot easier and less dangerous than being a fisherman, and much drier and warmer as well.

****** *George*

It was a warm day with great, billowing, white clouds overhead. I was daydreaming about being with Beth as I stood with my father and his lieutenants. We were watching archers who were waiting to board the two Company galleys that were approach the floating wharf in front of our training camp.

We would be boarding all of our galleys shortly and be gone for no one knows how long. The coast of Africa was a long way away, so we were likely to be gone for many months—and even longer if we took prizes that had to be sailed to Cyprus. At least that is what everyone was being told.

Beth had been greatly distressed about me leaving. I had just returned from taking her to Restormel. She will stay there with her sister and my mums and little sisters whilst I am away. No one would say for sure, but the archers and everyone else, including me, think we are about to sail for Tunis, or perhaps Algiers, to take prizes and answer the Pope's call to free their Christian slaves.

I was thinking of Beth and straining to hear what Harold was saying to my father when out of the corner of my eye I saw two of Raymond's outriders ride into camp. I watched as they made inquiries and then headed their horses straight to us.

We gathered around and listened as the outriders made their report. It seems another party of armed men with the coats of arms of some of the rebellious barons has avoided Ilchester by coming in from the north. They are at this moment moving down the road past Okehampton and bound for Exeter.

Harold and everyone else listened carefully to the outriders, and my father asked them quite a few questions before they knuckled their foreheads in salute and rode off to care for their horses and get something to eat and drink.

After they rode off, to my surprise, Harold complained about the archers on the quay being loaded too slowly. He told me go to the quay and let the sergeants know he wanted them to speed up. I was also to order another galley to be brought to the quay and be ready to take on its archers as soon as the galley now loading rowed away to wait in the estuary with all the others.

When the next two galleys finished loading, only Harold's galley would remain, the one my father and I and Harold would be on when we sailed for the Mediterranean.

These orders do not make sense, I thought as I jogged down to the quay. *Why are we still going after the Moors? Should not we be using our men to stop the barons from gathering at Rougemont as the King commanded us?*

Later that evening, Harold's galley was anchored with the other fully loaded galleys in the harbour. He and I were in the forecastle playing chess by the light of a candle lantern. That was when I asked him why we had ignored the barons traveling to Exeter and continued to load archers to take them to fight the Moors.

"Your father is a shrewd man, George. If we help the King totally defeat the barons, the King will not need us anymore to hold this part of England. Letting the barons assemble and then only partially defeating them or preventing the French from reinforcing themmeans the King will still need us. That is a good outcome so long as we kill the Earl of Devon and end up with Rougemont Castle and Exeter."

******

Not all of my father's lieutenants sailed with us to take Moorish prizes. Peter stayed behind to command the men my father left behind to protect Cornwall.

Raymond also did not sail with us even though many of his horse archers had been temporarily assigned to galleys as archers for the duration of our raid. He was staying behind at Okehampton as its captain and Peter's number two. Uncle Thomas was also not with us. Just before we sailed, he and Uncle Yoram had ridden off to London for some mysterious reason they would not share with anyone, not even their apprentice sergeants.

When I asked Francis, Uncle Thomas's apprentice sergeant, why he and my uncle were going to London, he said he did not know. Maybe he does know and will not say. Francis was jealous of me and the other boys that were going on the raid. He had never been outside of England, not even to Wales.

Uncle Yoram's absence was the most surprising. I would have thought he had been sailing with us since we will undoubtedly be going on to Cyprus with our prizes. Cyprus, after all, was where we usually send them.

******

Two days later, the weather in the channel looked good, and we were waiting in the Fowey estuary for the last of the sergeants captaining our galleys to finish climbing aboard Harold's galley. When they were all on board, my father was going to tell them our destination and Harold was going to give them their sailing orders.

My father had waited to announce our destination until the weather was good enough to cross the channel. We all understood and appreciated the reason for the delay. It was because they did not want word of our raid reaching the Moorish ports we were going to hit. I was thinking it would be Algiers and Tunis.

******

"Alright. Everyone listen up," my father shouted as he raised his arms to command everyone has attention and silence. The men crowding the deck of Harold galley, mostly four stripe sergeants captaining the galleys anchored all around us, went silent. What they heard next was not at all what anyone expected to hear.

"Many of you men think we are going after Moorish prizes. You are wrong. We are going after French prizes and a lot of them."

The men on the deck, including me, were truly gobsmacked. For a brief moment, there was a burst of gasps and oohs and aahs, then there were murmuring voices, and then cheers. *Everyone was pleased; we will be back to England or to wherever we are stationed a lot sooner than everyone expected.*

Once again, my father raised his hands to quiet the men. Then he explained.

"At this moment, King Phillip is assembling a huge fleet of French transports at Harfleur along with an army of soldiers and mercenaries for the fleet to carry to England to fight our King and take over England.

"Empty French transports are what we hope to find and take, but we cannot be sure they will be there. Lieutenant Henry has recently looked at them. He thinks if we hurry many of the French ships will be empty of men except for their sailors—but we would not know for sure until we get there and try to take them."

Lieutenant Henry? Did he just say Lieutenant Henry?

"But here is the thing. We are not going to do what we have done in the past and cut out a few prizes and sail off with them. This time we are going to stay in the harbour and in the river that runs up to Paris until we have taken or destroyed all of them, every damn one."

There was a dead silence for a few seconds as the words and their meaning sank in. The sergeant captains looked at each other in amazement. This was an opportunity for prizes and prize money beyond everyone has greatest dreams. Suddenly, there were great cheers from every man. I yelled until my throat went dry and my father finally raised his arms for quiet.

The sound of the sergeants' cheering rolled out over the harbour and estuary, and spirits rose everywhere among our anchored galleys. The men did not know what their captains had just heard, but they knew it was good and their spirits rose. Some of them even started cheering themselves, though they did not know why.

It was a while before my father could continue, even after he raised his arms.

After the cheering finally stopped, there were more than two hours of specific instructions and many questions from the captains. The questions were about such things as prize crews and rendezvous and when to withdraw and where to go when they did. A parchment map of France and the channel was handed to every sergeant captain to help him find his way.

We will row for France in the morning if the weather holds good.

I had wondered why Harold had me take his map and the blank parchments to Bodmin for the monks to copy and had me wait until they finished so I could bring them straight back; now I know.

Chapter Seventeen

Final preparations.

Our armada of Company war galleys lit the sky over the harbour that night in a way no one has ever before seen or probably ever would again. It was as if the stars overhead had come down to the water to twinkle at us and light the night. It all came about because of Harold's order for all galleys to stay close together. His purpose was simple: he wanted us all to fall upon the French at the same time when our raid began.

Harold's order was for every galley to hang all of its candle lanterns to show its location. The reason for flying all the lanterns was so our helmsmen could hold our fleet tightly together. As a result, the harbour sparkled with little points of light as far as the eye could see. It was as if the stars in the night sky had somehow fallen to earth.

I have never seen such a sight, and the veteran sailors and archers said they had not either. There seemed to be as many lights sparkling on the water as stars in the sky. We spent hours on deck just watching with delight. The lights flickered in the swells like the fireflies we sometimes saw in the marshes along the river.

Harold and I ate with my father and Randolph before Randolph went to his galley and my father turned in for the night. Harold was not inclined to sleep after the sergeant captains left to row their dinghies back to their galleys, so I could not sleep either. We played chess instead.

****** *George*

Harold and I played chess most of the night by the light of a swaying candle lantern as we listened to the creak of the galley's hull and the periodic calls of our lookouts when we got too close to another galley in the crowded harbour. I was not sure whether it was excitement about the coming battle or fears of a collision keeping us awake. Probably both.

"This is a good game for you if you are to captain the archers someday," Harold said with a sound of approval in his voice. "It was a game of war and Thomas was right to teach you and the other apprentices how to play it."

It shocked me when he said the words, and I sat up straight and studied at him closely. What he had just said was true, and it was the first time I realized it.

"Your father's the master of using the lessons of Chess. And here he goes again using the channel as his board. He is giving up a lot of this year's refugee and cargo coins to put the Company's fleet in place to protect King John from King Phillip's knights and bishops. Yes, he is. He is castling King John with our fleet to prevent King Phillip and his men from moving across the channel to knock over John.

"Your father is a sly old fox and a good captain and chess player, there are no two ways about it. We could have waited for Phillip to sail for England with his knights and tried to kill him in the channel with our galleys. Or, we could have waited until Phillip and his knights and soldiers got across the channel and helped John kill him with our archers and pike men.

"But he does not do either, does he? He is content to pass up the Moorish prizes and refugee coins we would have taken in order to protect King. Why? because he only wants to check King Phillip, not defeat him.

"He wants to leave Phillip standing so the game will continue."

"But how will the game end, Uncle Harold?"

"It will not end for a while, lad; no, it will not. Perhaps never and certainly not until the Company is rich enough and strong enough to take both kings and all their important men off the board at the same time and put the board away—as you and I had best do now so we can get some sleep."

******

We remained at anchor the next day as well, because the wind was wrong and the sky turned overcast. I could tell my father was anxious to leave, because he constantly paced the deck and seemed to consult our galley's parchment map every twenty minutes or so. But we stayed put because Harold kept insisting we should wait for better weather so our galleys could stay together and arrive at the same time.

Harold shook me awake the next morning about an hour before the early light of dawn. There was already a lot of quiet commotion on deck, and my father was already up. Through the open door, I saw him standing on the deck. My first thought, even before I headed to the shite nest to piss into the sea, was a question: is the weather good enough for us to risk the channel?

As soon as I stepped out onto the deck and smelled the morning bread being cooked, I knew we would be sailing that day. It was still dark, but the sky was clear and the stars were out, and I could feel the favourable wind.

Ten minutes later our rowers had finished eating, and I was standing in line with some of the remaining archers waiting for bread and a cut of cheese. That was when Harold ordered the "follow me" flag waved by the men in the lookout's nest up near the masthead and motioned for me to run up the mast and make sure it was done.

I was back down and standing with Harold when the rowing drums began to boom and we led our galleys out of the estuary. The sun was just starting to come up and the wind was from the west.

***** Galley captain William Wood

I made my mark on the Company list as William Wood because I had chopped firewood for Lord Anthony as one of his serfs before I went for an archer. I have been a four stripe sergeant ever since Captain William made me a prize captain and I took a galley off the Moors in Tunis and got it back to Cyprus. And I was fit to burst with excitement and anticipation as I rowed my dinghy back from the meeting with Captain William on Harold's galley, I surely was.

"Sorry, lads," I shouted to my men as they gathered around to get the news. "I know where we are heading, but I cannot tell you until we are clear of the estuary and well into the channel. Orders from the Captain himself because he does not want our enemies to know we are coming. And he is right; yes, he is. There is no sense taking a chance on the word getting out, is there?"

My men were veterans. They grumbled at the news but they were satisfied, as I knew they would be, because surprise is always best. They stayed calm as we waited the rest of that day and all the next for the Captain and Harold to decide the winds and weather were favourable enough for us to sail. It finally looked like it might be good enough on the second morning, and it was.

A few minutes after the sun came up there was a great hail from Alfred, my lookout up in the nest on the mast.

"Hoy, the deck; the Lieutenant Commander's galley has begun waving its 'follow me' flag and is beginning to hoist its sail."

It was the signal we had been waiting for and something I had been expecting—because the wind and weather felt good when I got up to piss in the middle of the night.

I followed Captain William's orders and waited until an hour after we entered the channel to tell the men where we are heading and what we are going to do. The men cheered loud enough to wake the dead when they heard. The landsmen on the lower rowing benches were already sea poxed, almost to a man, and even some of them smiled and whooped. I must admit I laid it on rather thick about the prize money and being back in England to spend it.

When I finished and things had calmed down a bit, I did as Captain William told us to do. I called the sergeants of my archers and sailors to me to help organize additional prize crews so we would be ready if we were able to take more than three prizes.

More prize crews means I will have to use some of the French and Norman French speakers in our crew and among our landsmen rowers as interpreters to tell the French crews we capture what we want them to do.

Then I will put archers on each additional prize to make damn sure they do it. We are also supposed to include at least one experienced sailor in each of our additional prize crews to make sure the French sailors actually set their sails properly and do whatever it is the prize crew tells them to do.

Chapter Eighteen

The battle begins

Being with my father and Uncle Harold in the command galley was quite pleasing. We spent all the next day moving down the channel towards Harfleur with our Company's fleet of war galleys following close behind. Fortunately, the sea was moderate. Even so, a good number of the men, myself included, were sea poxed and spent the day barfing over the side.

As the sun rolled on past in its great circle around the earth and darkness began to fall, Uncle Harold gave the order and we hoisted the coloured candle lights so the other galleys could mark us. Behind us we could see the flickering lights of our fleet.

All night the weather held and our galleys sailed and rowed together with our galley in the lead. I tried to sleep but I could not. Neither could my friend and fellow student Michael, my father's apprentice, with whom I shared a bed. The next morning, we were both wide awake and on deck before the sun came up.

"Excellent position, Harold. Absolutely excellent. Good on you and your pilots."

That was my father's enthusiastic, cheerful comment to Harold when our position in the channel became clear as the sun came up. They had climbed the mast together and were in the lookout's nest. I heard what he said because Michael and I were desperately clinging to the rope ladder below them as the ladder swung around and about and up and down in response to the wind and the waves.

I was pleased they were pleased, because I did not have a clue as to where we were and, truth be told, I was so sea poxed I hardly cared. All I could see was a long, grey blur to the south.

****** *George*

After my father and Harold decided they had seen enough, they climbed down from the mast. Then, whilst my father walked around inspecting everyone's weapons and looking once again at the arrows in the bales, I followed Harold as he prowled every corner of the galley and made sure everyone had eaten all the bread and cheese they wanted and received two full bowls of breakfast ale.

Archers and sailors briefly took the place of the landsmen on the lower rowing deck so they too could break their nightly fast. There was obviously some trading going on, as I saw several men that had obviously had too much morning ale to drink.

To my surprise, most of the archers, and especially the older men, curled up on whatever vacant space they could find and went right back to sleep after they finished pissing and breaking their nightly fast.

When I mentioned this to Uncle Harold, he told me it is quite common for veteran fighting men to sleep whenever they have time to do so. He told me it was a good thing to see. It meant the men knew what they were doing and were resigned to carrying out their assignments and accepting whatever their fate would be.

******

"Hoy, the deck! Sail in sight dead ahead." It was a hail from the lookouts, and we heard similar ones repeated more and more often as we moved towards Harfleur. Usually it meant one or more fishing boats, but on four occasions it was an inbound transport with its sails set to catch the prevailing wind. We never did see any outbound shipping other than many small fishing boats, which we ignored.

Harold and I would climb the mast each time a large transport was reported by our lookouts. If it was big enough, Harold would order a flag waved by one of the lookouts, and one or more of the galleys behind us would peel off from our armada to take it as a prize.

After a while, I noticed the responding galley was never one of the galleys immediately behind ours.

Harold explained why when I asked.

"The galleys right behind us cannot go traipsing off to fetch prizes, no they cannot. They have got to stay up with us, because they will be coming with us all the way to the quay to help take the cogs and ships moored along it."

* * * * * *

About four hours after sunrise came the hail, "Hoy, the deck! Many masts in sight dead ahead."

Harold and my father ran to the mast and climbed up to the lookout's nest to see for themselves. Michael and I followed right behind them, as was our duty.

Suddenly, there they were in front of our eyes, a virtual forest of masts. It was the French fleet at anchor in Harfleur harbour. A few moments later, a command came from Harold to slightly change the direction our galley was sailing and slightly increase our speed.

Almost instantly our rowing drum began to beat a somewhat faster tune. Soon thereafter sergeants began shouting, and the archers and boarding parties began looking to their weapons and forming up in their assigned positions. It was quite familiar after all of the practices I had watched, but this time, somehow, it was quite thrilling. I suddenly very much needed to piss and shite. *How strange.*

******

Michael and I quickly climbed down the rope ladder and moved out of the way when both my father and Uncle Harold motioned for us to do so and started down themselves.

"Fetch your bows and quivers, lads, and the captain's, too," was the first thing Harold said as his feet touched the deck. "And fetch me my sword and a shield." We scampered to obey.

It seemed as if no time at all had passed before we entered the crowded harbour at Harfleur and began rowing for the long, stone quay that seemed to run all along the front of the city wall. The harbour was packed with cargo transports and large fishing boats at anchor. Harold had our rowing drum reduce its beat to a crawl and added another rudder man as we slowly weaved through the densely packed harbour towards the quay.

Men on the French transports looked down at us as we rowed our way past them. A few of them even waved and nodded. They had no idea as to who we were or the horror we were about to lay upon them. It was exhilarating.

******

Michael and I stood next to Harold and my father on the roof of the forecastle, ready to carry out any order or run any errand they might require of us. Both of us clutched our bows and an arrow with one hand and used the other to steady ourselves against the wooden railing circling the roof, as did the half dozen archers crowded on the deck with us. I suddenly realized I was holding my bow so tightly my fingers were getting numb.

From our vantage point we could look down upon our galley's deck about six feet below us. It was crowded with the men of our boarding parties. They too were anxiously holding their weapons and constantly peering at the French transports we were passing. I could see more than a dozen archers in the stern. Every man's longbow was strung.

Our men and galleys reminded me of a great arrow being readied for Harold and my father to launch against the unsuspecting French.

It gave me a great start and a strange pleasure when I suddenly realized I had been thinking in terms of arrows. At that moment, I knew for sure I had become an archer like my father.

What surprised me was the silent intensity of the men around me and on the deck just below me. I did not remember an order being issued for everyone to be silent, but it must have been given. Perhaps no one wanted to attract attention from the enemy transports we were passing. It was a mystery.

Everyone clutched their weapons and watched silently as we moved toward the quay. Our galley's oars slowly splashed and swooshed as we turned and twisted this way and that to get through the extremely crowded and totally disorganized harbour.

The rowing drum had long since ceased to beat. The landsmen on the lower rowing deck and the rudder men were pulling their oars in response to the periodic orders being shouted down from the sailing sergeant on our galley's stubby mast.

Other than the sailing sergeant's voice and the voices of the rowing sergeant repeating them, the only sounds on our galley were the creak of its wooden hull and the swoosh of our oars. It was a difficult passage. More than once we came so close to a French transport that our oars had to be hurriedly pulled in to avoid being sheared off.

After tense minutes and more than a few near collisions, we finally approached the long quay and the line of French transports moored along it. We turned to the right and began to row along the moored transports towards the far end of the quay. An open berth at the far end was obviously where Harold intended to unload our prize crews.

When I looked backwards past our stern castle and shite nest, I could see some of our galleys following behind us. They would put their prize crews ashore in other open mooring berths even if it means they had to create a berth for themselves by forcing their bows in between two French transports and unloading their prize crews over their bows.

Our men had every right to be tense. The French cogs and ships we rowed past in the harbour may have been almost empty of men, but some of those on the quay where our prize crews would be landing were packed with French soldiers and mercenaries and many more were standing and sitting on the quay preparing to board the transports moored all along it.

We could hear the shouts and talking of the French troops on the quay whenever we rowed past an opening between the anchored transports. They paid no attention to us except as a curiosity; war galleys such as ours are not common in these waters.

Everything changed as we began moving past a large, two-masted transport moored close to the empty berth we were heading for at the far end of the quay. Unlike the other transports in the harbour, this one's deck was crowded with French soldiers staring across at us from no more than thirty paces away.

The transport's deck was six or seven feet higher than our galley's deck. As a result, the archers and boarding parties standing on our deck could only see the soldiers and sailors on the French transport that were standing along its deck railing and looking down at them. We on the roofs of our galley's castles, on the other hand, were high enough to be able to see the French ship's entire deck.

We could clearly see the looks on the faces of the French soldiers as their expressions turned from curiosity to stunned surprise. There immediately began to be shouting and confusion on the transport's deck.

Some of the French soldiers gaped at us as we slowly moved past them and a few dove for cover. There were obviously veterans among them who knew what it meant when they saw archers with bows strung and arrows in their hands. What they did not know was whether we were friend or foe and what our intentions might be.

The distance between where I was standing on the roof of the forecastle and the hull of the troop-laden French transport was barely enough to get our oars in the water, perhaps twenty paces. There was a young Frenchman with a drooping moustache at its railing, staring at us as we glided past. Our eyes locked, and for some reason I raised my hand in acknowledgement and nodded. He nodded back. Neither of us smiled.

******

I stood behind my father and Harold and watched as we slowly moved into the open berth at the end of the quay. This end of the quay was absolutely packed with French soldiers and mercenaries boarding or preparing to board the French transports moored in the nearby berths—and many of them were staring at us as we approached the quay.

We attracted the attention of the French soldiers because of our men's behaviour. Harold had responded to the cries of alarm from the soldiers on the deck of one of the transports by ordering our men to put their weapons down at their feet and pretend to smile and look friendly. Some of them obviously overdid it by smiling and waving too much. It drew more attention and curiosity from the soldiers crowded together on this end of the quay than if the order had not been given at all. *I need to remember that.*

In any event, it was a gentle mooring as the linen-filled bumper sacks hanging over the side of our galley prevented us from banging up against the quay and doing our galley an injury.

Everything changed the moment our galley touched the quay, because the gentle bump was the signal for the archers on our deck and castle roofs to pick up their bows and begin pushing out their arrows and for the non-archers in our boarding parties to grab up their swords and galley shields and begin climbing onto the quay.

One moment there was the relative peace and quiet and bustling about one might expect from a mass of soldiers standing with their supplies and personal possessions as they waited to board their transports; the next moment there were screams and a scene of chaos and utter confusion as a rapidly increasing hail of well-aimed arrows began to fall upon them.

For a moment, many of the Frenchmen on the quay just stood there in a daze and stared at us. They did not even know where the deadly storm of arrows was coming from. Then those that still could began to scream and scatter.

I stood next to my father on the forecastle roof as we and the archers around us pushed arrow after arrow into the screaming and totally confused French soldiers. They did not know where to run, and they were not wearing armour. We slaughtered them.

Chapter Nineteen

A great sea battle.

I stood next to my son and fought as an archer once the fighting started. It seemed as if our surprise attack on the French soldiers went on forever, but it was actually over in less than a minute. Our archers were within spitting distance of the screaming and totally disorganized French soldiers and trained to shoot accurately. We shot them down in droves as our sword- and shield-carrying sailors and the other non-archers in our landing parties quickly placed their boarding ladders and began scrambling up them to reach the quay.

I remember one of the French soldiers on the quay quite clearly. He was looking at us and paused to pick up a bundle of his possessions when the shouting and commotion started around him and we began shooting. My arrow caught him square in the middle of his chest and caused him to take a step backward. In the brief moment whilst I was nocking my next arrow, I saw him look down at the protruding shaft in surprise and watched as his expression changed to one of horror and disbelief.

Our storm of arrows quickly cleared our section of the quay of standing Frenchmen. Most were either down with arrows in them or cowering on the ground and trying to hide by the time the archers in our boarding parties began following the sword- and pike-carrying non-archers up the boarding ladders and into the chaos and confusion and noise on the quay.

The French soldiers that cowered should have run. The men in our boarding parties knew full well they could not afford to leave able-bodied fighting men in their rear—and they did not despite the cowering men's desperate pleas and attempts to surrender.

Less than a minute after we bumped against the quay, our boarding parties had begun to board the French cogs and ships moored nearby, and our galley's main deck was clear of everyone except the sailors holding us against the quay with the hooks on their bladed pikes.

Those of us on the castle roof remained engaged despite our boarding parties' initial successes. Not all of the running and screaming and hiding Frenchmen on the quay had been killed as the men in our boarding parties ran past them. Many of them were still running about and moving and drawing our attention and arrows as they did.

I never did give an order to stop shooting. Everything just tailed off as we ran out of targets.

****** William

From the roof of the forecastle where my son and I were standing, I could see and hear the progress of our boarding parties and prize crews on the quay and in the harbour. We had taken the French by surprise, and there was no doubt about it. Already our prize crews were starting to raise the anchors and sails of some of the transports in the harbour in preparation for sailing them to London.

The situation was much the same here at Harfleur's long quay. The prize crew on the two-masted transport to my right had already cast off its mooring lines and was starting to raise its sails, despite some of its crew jumping off its deck and onto the quay in a desperate effort to escape. Some did escape; others drew an unnecessary arrow.

There was trouble, however, three berths down to my left. Our boarding party was meeting resistance on the big three-masted transport we had passed earlier, the one that appeared to have already loaded some of its soldiers.

I would have sent reinforcements running down the quay to help them if I could, but the Frenchman's mooring lines had been cut or cast off, and it was beginning to drift away. The ship was out of control with our prize crew and archers on board and in serious trouble.

Pushing away from the quay and rowing out to the aid of our boarding party turned out to be unexpectedly difficult and time-consuming. Our sailors had trouble pushing us far enough away from the quay with their pikes so we could get our quayside oars into the water and begin moving towards the drifting ship.

The brief delay was all it took to turn a problem into a serious crisis. Now our only chance of saving our prize crew was to reinforce them by boarding the drifting Frenchman in the harbour, just as we would if we encountered it out in the ocean. It was very distressing.

****** George

My father got very upset when we had trouble getting our quayside oars into the water. I started to say something to him when Harold shouted out an order sending Michael and me scurrying up to the lookout's nest with our bows to join the two archers already up there. Two of Harold's sailors were assigned to carry arrows up to the four of us. I never did know their names.

"Go up there and help the archers pick them off!" Harold roared. "John from London's prize crew and the archers on yonder Frenchman's deck are in trouble. We have got to support them. Hurry, lads, hurry!"

Michael and I ran to the mast and scrambled up the rope ladder to the nest. When we arrived we could see my father and some archers getting ready to shoot from the roof of the stern castle and Harold preparing to lead a boarding party consisting of every sailor remaining on our galley, even the sailing sergeant and the rowing sergeant and the cook.

We could see a small, desperate band of our men on the transport's deck. They were backed into a defensive position in the bow and being assaulted by a much larger group of Frenchmen. There were dead and wounded men all over the deck. Some of them were wearing Company tunics.

Chapter Twenty

The Company Captain.

I am Edward from Ditchling on the rolls of the Company of Archers and I have been the captain of galley number sixteen ever since Captain William made me up to be the sergeant captain of the prize crew that took it out of Tunis when it was almost new.

Number sixteen was now old and leaked a bit but she was a sturdy, double-masted, eighty-oar galley with two rowing decks and a new leather sail. We sailed from Cornwall with twelve sailor men on board along with seventy-two archers and forty-seven sea poxed landsmen on the lower benches to do the rowing and bail the water.

My sailing sergeant and pilot was old, white-haired Jack that had been a draper's apprentice in London before running off to sea many years ago before Richard was king. Jack kept us close together with the other galleys, and we spent the entire day following Harold's command galley down the channel. *Jack Draper had been the three-stripe sergeant of my sailors and my pilot for years, ever since we were sergeants on the prize crew that took our galley from the Moors.*

That evening, we once again hung out all our candle lamps and continued to make good time even though the wind fell off a bit after dark. As you can well imagine, Jack and my other sergeants and I and my lookouts stayed awake all night as the landsmen took turns rowing on our lower bank of oars. Jack had his sailors continually adjust the sail to get the most we could from the wind in order to rest our rowers and still be able to stay with the fleet.

There were galley lights twinkling all around us and galleys in the fleet stayed close—too close to my way of thinking. Two or three times we almost collided with another galley, and once we actually took a minor hit and broke a couple oars when we scraped against Bill Owen's Number Forty-one

Our fleet looked to still be together the next morning. We were in the middle of the channel and already well past the Pointe de Barfleur when the sun came creeping up over the far end of the earth. I had climbed the mast and been up there in the nest to be able to see our position for myself. I would wager every captain in our fleet was on his mast waiting for the sun to arrive just like me.

What we saw was quite encouraging, though we had sailed too far to the east in the darkness. Harold's desire to keep us together and safe from running aground had kept us more towards the middle of the channel than some of us might have preferred. All in all, however, our position was quite acceptable. We were well placed and safe, ready to move towards Harfleur where we had been told the French fleet was about to board French soldiers to invade England..

Harold turned his galley south to lead us towards the French fleet as soon as the sun rolled up over the horizon enough for him to see the shore and fix our position. Our still-sea poxed lower deck landsmen soon settled into the steady rate of rowing needed to stay in the middle of our fleet; our archers and boarding parties began opening their arrow bales and laying out their arrows, swords, and bladed pikes.

After a while, I sent the men to breakfast and made sure they each had two bowls of morning ale and all the bread and cheese they wanted to eat. Some of them got sea poxed but most of them seemed to feel better for the meal and the extra ale. I know I did.

We had hoped to reach Harfleur's big harbour and its long stone quay about three hours after sunup. It was not to be. We were too far east. Jack said it would most likely take us four or five hours to reach the French transports we had been told are assembling to carry the French army to England. We agreed it would not be a problem; we would have more than enough hours of daylight to attack the French ships and take prizes.

The best news was our fleet of war galleys appeared to have stayed together and safe in the night. It meant we would be able to hit the French with one mighty blow and get rich from all the prizes. I shared the good news with my archers and sailors as I walked about the decks.

Some of the sea poxed men were obviously more interested in getting ashore than anything else. Most of the archers and sailors, however, seemed to be quite anxious for the fighting to begin. I certainly was.

Everywhere there was talking as the men examined their arrows and bows and used the smooth river stones each of our galleys carries so they can sharpen their blades and arrowheads. I began sharpening mine when I returned to the roof of the stern castle after a brief visit to the shite nest hanging over the stern.

****** *Edward Ditchling*

Almost immediately upon turning south to follow Harold's galley, my lookouts on the mast began to report seeing potential prizes and a number of large fishing boats. The French transports did not even attempt to flee; their captains probably thought we were coming to join the French invasion fleet. In a manner of speaking, we were.

My crew and I watched intently and with more than a bit of jealousy as one of the galleys behind us turned and began rowing hard towards the first of our armada's potential prizes. She was a big, inbound, two-masted cog riding high in the water to indicate she was empty. She was almost certainly a transport coming in to help carry the French army to England.

Our prize crews were to sail for either London or Cornwall, depending on the wind and weather. If the weather was bad, they were to wait until their prize sergeants thought it good enough for them to be able to reach one or the other. At that moment, the wind and weather favoured London, but it could change in an instant; one could never be sure about the weather in the Channel.

******

We followed Harold Lewes's command galley and, suddenly, we could see Harfleur on the horizon. As we got closer, we could see the city's harbour was packed with shipping. There were more potential prizes in sight than you could possibly imagine.

My galley's particular assignment was to be one of the three galleys following Harold's galley to the Harfleur quay, and to join it in taking prizes from among the French transports moored along it.

At first, we had trouble keeping up with the command galley as we rowed towards the harbour entrance. Harold had suddenly begun moving faster for some reason. We were still using only our landsmen as rowers. They were all on the lower deck and doing their best. Even so, it was all we could do to keep Harold's galley in sight and follow him as he weaved in and out among the numerous French bottoms.

My initial reaction was one of excitement and wonder at all the French shipping, but I could not understand why Harold and Captain William were in such a great hurry. The Frenchies were not going anywhere, and we were at great risk of collision.

We did not find and move into an open mooring space on the Harfleur quay at exactly the same moment as Harold's galley, but we reached one shortly thereafter because Harold went for an open space at the most distant end of the quay and had a further distance to row. Maybe they were rowing so hard so that we would arrive at the quay at the same time.

"Back oars! Back oars!" my rowing sergeant, Charlie, yelled to our rowers as we surged towards an open space on the Harfleur quay about six hundred paces south of where Harold's galley had just moored. We were lucky to find an open space, though the quay was quite large and had many berths. There were French transports tied up all along it.

I climbed down from the lookout's nest to make room for more archers and trotted down the deck to stand on the roof of the stern castle with a dozen or more of my best archers and Jack.

****** *Captain Ditchling*

Harold's archers on the command galley were already pushing out arrows at the men on the quay as we moved into the vacant mooring position. My archers and I had helped by adding our arrows to those falling on the French as soon as we got close enough to reach them. We grabbed up and pushed out arrows from the bales we had opened on the galley deck so we could keep our quivers full.

We could see great confusion on the quay as we approached it. There were men running about in every direction and wounded men on the ground or trying to stagger away to safety. Some among the French obviously did not know what to do and were cowering on the ground.

For a few moments after the first hailstorm of arrows began to land, some of the French soldiers were still trying to gather up the personal effects they had obviously intended to carry aboard the transports with them. Their efforts did not last long. With men dropping all around them, the French soldiers soon realized their only choice was to either cower on the ground and play dead or run through our storm of arrows and try to escape. If they just stood there, they would die for sure.

Of course, they ran. They may be French and eat snails and give each other disgusting poxes, but no one wants to die if he can avoid it.

Until our galleys arrived and the arrows started flying, the French soldiers had obviously been boarding or preparing to board the transport ships moored along the quay.

Our arrival caused the unsuspecting Frenchmen to quickly fall into a state of total confusion. They began running about on the quay in all directions, and there was a great deal of shouting and screaming and noise both from the men on my galley and from the Frenchmen on the quay and the transports moored all along it.

One thing was clear—the French soldiers on the quay were totally confused, surprised, disorganized, and leaderless.

******

Most of the unwounded French soldiers had escaped by the time Jack brought our old Number Sixteen up against the quay. We hit it so hard several of the archers around me fell off the roof of the castle and landed on the deck. Jack and I and some of the archers standing with us on the roof saw it coming and braced ourselves. Even so, I went to my knees and only avoided smashing my nose by dropping my bow and throwing out both hands to break my fall.

Some of the archers on the castle roof with me were not so lucky. They had been rightly concentrating on shooting Frenchmen and were taken by surprise when we crashed into the quay. The railing around the castle roof broke from the weight of the men thrown against it, and several of them fell off the roof. One of them did not get up immediately, but at least he was alive and trying to sit up; he was lucky not to have gone into the water and drowned.

At least, thank God for his mercy, none of my archers in the lookout's nest came down. Falling from the castle roof to the deck is one thing; falling from the lookout's nest to the deck is something else.

For some reason, and despite all the chaos and noise around me, being knocked off my feet and seeing the men around me fly forward when we hit the quay made me think of how enemy knights fly off into the air when the grounded pikes of our archers abruptly stop their horses. Just going to my knees when we hit the quay was unsettling; I can only imagine what it must be like to fly through the air wearing armour and land with a crash in the middle of a large number of enemy soldiers. *And I certainly did not want to find out. What I have heard is that it is almost always fatal either from the fall or from being stabbed by the pissed off enemy soldiers you land on.*

******

My archers and prize crews were waiting impatiently and quickly recovered from the chaos caused by our hard arrival. They did not have to wait for our galley to finish being moored to the quay, because it would not happen. Jack had sailors standing along the deck railing using the hooks on the blades of their long pikes to hold us against the quay. This allowed for a fast departure if we had to run.

There was much swearing and yelling as my men picked themselves up from the deck and began climbing onto my galley's railing. From there, they pulled themselves onto the quay. Others used our boarding ladders, that had been deployed and waiting in case our galley's deck was too far below the quay. All the while, the archers and I poured arrows into the few panic-stricken Frenchmen we could see on the quay.

Within seconds, the men of our prize crews were running unmolested along the quay to get to the transports moored on either side of us. As they did they were finishing off the wounded French soldiers as they ran past them on their way to board the French transports and take them as prizes.

As we rowed up I had counted thirteen French transports moored along the quay. Now Harold's galley and two of our other galleys and mine were up against the quay and unloading their prize crews.

Only one of our galleys intended for the quay, my good friend Richard's, had not yet disembarked its prize crews. The quay was so crowded with ships that Richard could not find enough space to even get his galley's bow in to unload his men, let alone enough room to come in alongside it.

Richard thought quickly when he found no room along the quay; I will give him that. His prize crews immediately began boarding one of the French ships on its seaward side. Richard's intention was obvious—to take the Frenchman and send the rest of his prize crews and archers across its deck to reach the quay and the rest of the French shipping tied up in the berths along it.

Richard must be furious. He will never hear the end of it, would he? Arriving last and finding no place to land his men, I mean.

Chapter Twenty-one
Victory and despair.

I was a free man from a manor south of Walsall when I made my mark on the Company's rolls years ago at Acre as Andrew of the woods. There were already a number of Andrews in the Company, so they added "wood" to my name because my father laboured for Sir Robert as his gamekeeper and woodcutter before I ran away to go for a crusader. I made my mark and joined the archers in the early days when the Company was first beginning to recruit men to replace its heavy losses in the crusade. I got my galley when I was the prize captain that took it out of Tunis and got it to Malta.

My galley was one of the three assigned to damage the French fishing boats before we start trying to take prizes. We were not to destroy them, only to temporarily damage them by using our axes to chop a plank out of each hull so it could not be used to carry French soldiers out to reinforce the French shipping anchored in the harbour.

According to Captain William, our spies said most of the fishing boats could be found along the beach to the north of the quay and the rest along the beach to the north of the harbour. So that is where we headed— to the beach just north of the harbour where the fishermen bring in their catches and beach their boats.

Normally we would have left the French fishing boats alone. But today was different; it was not the fishing grounds where they would soon be headed, it was England.

We followed Harold and the main force of our galleys until we reached the entrance to the crowded harbour. When they turned and entered the harbour, my galley and two others kept going until we had gone past the northern side of the stone jetty that helped enclose and protect it. Then we turned to our right and headed towards the fishing boats. A few seemed to be anchored just off the shore, but most were pulled up on the beach immediately next to the harbour.

We were the first to arrive, and many of the men and women on and around the fishing boats looked up as we approached. No one seemed particularly alarmed, even when the bow of my galley nudged the sandy bottom just before the shoreline. They appeared more curious than anything else.

Everything changed when my men began to pour over the bow of my galley into the knee-deep water and splashed ashore with axes and swords in their hands and shouting their battle cries. At first the people on the beach just stood there and gaped at us. Then they began screaming and running.

My men ignored the people and made straight for the fishing boats. There were quite a few of them on the beach, certainly more than we expected. It took more time than I had hoped for my men to finish temporarily disabling each of them with a few well-placed chops of an axe to their hulls. Not a single man or woman on the beach was touched. My men were under strict orders not to hurt them, only to disable their boats so they could not be used to ferry soldiers out to help defend the French shipping in the harbour.

I stood at the bow and counted my men as they came running back. When the last laggard jumped aboard, the four sailor men I had waiting in the water pushed us off and jumped back on board themselves. It was time to go back to the harbour entrance and block it so none of the Frenchies could escape.

I had heard Captain William say we would stay in the harbour overnight if that is what it took to take or burn all of the French shipping. Even so, my men and I were anxious to get to the harbour entrance and begin doing our share to increase the prize money that would be divided amongst us.

Without my having to say a word, all the oars on both banks of seats were manned by the time we had spun around and began moving down the long stone jetty towards the entrance to the harbour. Our rowing drum beat faster and faster.

******

Blocking the harbour entrance and taking any Frenchmen that tried to escape was our next assignment, and we barely reached it in time. A big three-masted Frenchman was coming out of the harbour and heading towards deep water as we came around the jetty. A number of sailors were on its deck and rigging, They were scrambling to set its sails and escape.

Most importantly, I could not see a single man on its deck that looked like one of ours, and there was certainly no one from one of our prize crews standing in its bow or stern rolling one of his arms in a great cranking motion to signal it was a prize. It was a French ship for sure, and it was trying to escape.

"She is a Frenchy, Jimmy, a three-master. Lay us alongside her and be quick about it," I yelled to my sailing sergeant.

"Boarders and first prize crew to the deck and prepare to board; archers to their boarding positions and stand by to push."

Then I repeated my order for good measure.

Within seconds, several dozen of my sailors and boarders were standing around me with their weapons and boarding ladders in hand. Archers were on the roofs of our castles preparing to support them by killing everyone they could see, and my sailors were readying their grappling hooks for throwing.

Boarding a prize was something my crew and I had practiced many hundreds of times. This time it would be for real.

******

Jimmy brought us alongside the French ship, and our grappling hooks went over the Frenchman's railing and were pulled tight by the sailors.

Up went our boarding ladders, and our prize crew and extra boarders promptly climbed them and took the French ship as a prize. There was no fighting. The French sailors were not fighting men and were not even armed. To the contrary, they were scared to death and willing to do whatever they were told.

Jimmy and I went up to the Frenchman's deck to get things organized as soon as our boarders secured control of the ship and began coming back down the ladders. The archers brought the transport's captain and his two mates down with them, as well as its bosun and two members of its crew that looked to be a bit tougher and more determined than the others.

Two of our sailors and six archers carrying swords and shields in addition to their bows took their places, along with one of our sea-poxed landsmen that could jabber French. They would be the prize crew; the French sailors we left on board would work the ship—or else.

Jimmy and I spent only a few minutes looking through the French ship and ordering its prize crew to make for London because of the wind. Then we rushed back down to our galley and moved off to once again block the harbour entrance and, hopefully, find another prize.

I do not know about Jimmy, but I for one was damn glad to get back to my galley. What we found was a fairly new and incredibly filthy ship quite capable of making London or Cornwall. I had never been on a French ship before. I had heard Jimmy and the sailors say they were always filthy, but I had not really believed it until I saw it for myself.

Harold would have had a fit. There was no shite nest behind the stern. The men apparently just pissed and shite wherever they happened to be when they felt the urge. It smelled as bad below deck as a Moorish slaver or the Templars I had met that never wiped their arses or washed their clothes in order to live as much as possible like Jesus who, being a God, never had to do such things.

******

All afternoon the amount of French shipping in the harbour slowly fell as more and more prizes were taken and passed through the harbour entrance on their way to London. As far as I could tell, not a one had escaped.

My galley had already taken three more prizes, and it was getting late in the day. There were still a number of French ships remaining in the harbour. Many of them were abandoned, their panic-stricken crews having taken to their small boats and rowed ashore before our prize crews could board them.

"My God, Jimmy! Look at how many are still there. We will be out of prize crews and have to start burning them soon."

"Sergeant! Sergeant!" one of my sailors suddenly called with an anxious sound in his voice. "Harold's galley started waving its 'form on me' flag, and then it came down."

"How long did you see it waving before it stopped?"

"That is just it, Sergeant. It started waving, but it did not just stop. It seemed to fall."

****** William

Our effort to come to the aid of our prize crew and boarding party fighting the French troops on the transport's deck started too slowly and almost ended disastrously. Some of our men on the Frenchy were already down by the time we finally pushed off from the quay and were able to start rowing towards the desperate fighting we could see and hear.

We finally were able to push off from the quay, but we were pointed in the wrong direction and hemmed in by the densely packed shipping. We did not have room to turn around where we were moored.

Our only option was to row through the ships in the harbour in a great curve so we could come back towards the French transport where the fighting was occurring. Doing so was made even more difficult because everywhere around us our galleys were boarding the anchored French transports, and numerous small dinghies were in the water as the French crews tried to escape from their doomed transports.

The collision with one of our own prizes was probably inevitable. Our men were rowing hard, and we were going fast as we came around a big French transport and did not see the French cog coming towards us until it was too late.

We collided so hard everyone on our deck was knocked off his feet and many of our rowers came off their benches. There was serious damage. Our bow was crushed and our mast, with George and its three other archers in the lookout's nest, whipped forward and snapped some of the strands of the heavy rope stays holding it up.

Fortunately, none of the archers were thrown out of the nest, though some of their arrows came raining down on our deck. Harold quickly gave the necessary orders. The deck crew began bailing out the water as it came in through our crushed bow, and another bale of arrows was quickly carried up to the nest as we once again rowed hard in a desperate effort to get back to our embattled prize crew.

****** *William*

We arrived too late to save most of the prize crew. George and the other archers in the nest began launching their arrows as soon as they could find targets, and those of us on the roofs of the castles soon joined them.

It was not hard to find targets; everyone on the French transport's packed deck was French except for the half dozen or so of our men still standing. They were fighting in a little defensive cluster in a corner near the front of the ship. From all the bodies in front of them, it appeared they had been giving a good account of themselves despite being hopelessly outnumbered.

Things only began to change when our arrows began raining down and taking the French soldiers on the deck. One after another the Frenchmen either went down to one of our arrows or ran below to escape.

When we got alongside, Harold and I raised the boarding ladders ourselves and led what was left of our sailors and archers up them whilst our archers in the lookout's nest and on the castle roofs kept watch.

We were too late. Only four of our men were still standing, and every man of them was wounded. We also found three of our men seriously wounded among the men that were down on the deck.

It took us quite a while to get our wounded men down the boarding ladders and onto our deck. It was something we had not practiced and we did it poorly. In the end, we put a mooring line under the arms of several of our strongest men, and they carried our wounded down the ladders as those of us above them let out the line and men below guided their feet and pushed on their arses so they would not come tumbling down. It was quite painful for some of our wounded. Several of them shrieked and screamed all the way down.

There was no way we could ever sail away with the French transport. With our prize crews already away on other prizes, we did not have enough sailors left to handle its sails.

Moreover, there was the not insignificant problem of it having hundreds of French soldiers on board that were likely to come on deck and retake it as soon as our archers were not nearby to kill them. So we did the next best thing—we set it on fire, rowing away only after the fire was raging and our last volunteer had scurried down the one remaining boarding ladder.

Desperate French soldiers began pouring out of the hold and jumping onto the quay and into the war as we left. We did not push arrows at them.

***** William

We spent the rest of the afternoon watching our galleys take prizes in the harbour, bailing the water coming in through our staved-in bow, and trying to make repairs so we could row away to safety. We might have succeeded if we could have beached the galley, but beaching it in France is the one thing we could not do. The French would have caught us and chopped our necks for sure.

In the end, Harold and I just looked at each other, and I ordered the men in the lookout's nest to wave the "form on me" flag at our nearest galleys. The sun was finishing its daily pass overhead, and the harbour was almost empty of ships except for our galleys and French ships being burned because we had no prize crews left to sail them away. It was time for Harold and I to transfer our men to another galley before the damn thing sunk out from under us.

One of our galleys came alongside in response to our signal and Harold's vigorous arm waving and bumped us a bit hard. As it did, I heard the loud *snap* as one of the stays broke and watched in horror as our mast slowly tipped over and fell into the sea carrying my son and all my dreams.

Epilogue

Our prizes continued arriving in London for days. It was a great victory and the King and William Marshal came to see them for themselves and thank us. The French fleet had been well and truly destroyed, and there would certainly be no invasion this year even though the barons were still gathering and were expected to fight without them.

Thomas was there too. He had ridden to London as soon as we sailed, and I was more than a little emotional when I saw him.

"The best thing you ever did was teach George and the boys how to swim," I told him.

***** The End *****

There are more books in *The Company of Archers Saga*.

All of the books in this great saga of medieval England are also available as individual eBooks, and some of them are also available in print and as audio books and multi-book collections. You can find them by searching for *Martin Archer stories.*

A bargain-priced collection of the entire first six books of the saga is available as *The Archers' Story.* Similarly, the three novels that follow the stories in the collection you just read are available as *The Archers' Story Part III;* and the four after that as *The Archers' Story: Part IV.* And there are more.

A chronological list of all the books in the saga, and other books by Martin Archer, can be found below.

Finally, a word from Martin:

"I sincerely hope you enjoyed reading the latest stories about my ancestors as much as I enjoyed writing them. If so, I respectfully request a favourable review on with as many stars as possible in order to encourage other readers.

"And, if you could please spare a moment, I would also very much appreciate your thoughts about this saga of medieval England, and whether you would like to see it continue. I can be reached at martinarcherV@gmail.com."

Cheers and thank you once again. /S/ Martin Archer

eBooks in the exciting and action-packed *The Company of Archers* saga:

The Archers

The Archers' Castle

The Archers' Return

The Archers' War

Rescuing the Hostages

Archers and Crusaders

The Archers' Gold

The Missing Treasure

Castling the King

The Sea Warriors

The Captain's Men

Gulling the Kings

The Magna Carta Decision

The War of the Kings

The Company's Revenge

The Ransom

The New Commander

The Gold Coins

The Emperor has no Gold

Fatal Mistakes

The Alchemist's Revenge

The Venetian Gambit

eBooks in Martin Archer's epic *Soldiers and Marines* saga:

Soldiers and Marines

Peace and Conflict

War Breaks Out

War in the East

Israel's Next War (A prescient book much hated by Islamic reviewers)

eBook Collections on Amazon

The Archers Stories I—complete books I, II, III, IV, V, VI

The Archers Stories II—complete books VII, VIII, IX, X,

The Archers Stories III—complete books XI, XII, XIII

The Archers Stories IV – complete books XIV, XV, XVI, XVII

The Soldiers and Marines Saga—complete books I, II, III

Other eBooks you might enjoy:

Cage's Crew by Martin Archer writing as Raymond Casey

America's Next War by Michael Cameron – an adaption of Martin Archer's *War Breaks Out* to set it in the immediate future when Eastern and Western Europe go to war over another wave of Islamic refugees.

Sample Pages from Book One – *The Archers*

.... We sometimes had to shoulder our way through the crowded streets and push people away as we walked towards the church. Beggars and desperate women and young boys began pulling on our clothes and crying out to us. In the distance black smoke was rising from somewhere in the city, probably from looters torching somebody's house or a merchant's stall.

The doors to the front of the old stone church were closed. Through the cracks in the wooden doors we could see the heavy wooden bar holding them shut.

"Come on. There must be a side door for the priests to use. There always is."

We walked around to the side of the church and there it was. I began banging on the door. After a while, a muffled voice on the other side told us to go away.

"The church is not open." The voice said.

"We have come from Lord Edmund to see the Bishop of Damascus. Let us in."

We could hear something being moved and then an eye appeared at the peep hole in the door. A few seconds later, the door swung open and we hurried in.

The light inside the room was dim because the windows were shuttered.

Our greeter was a slender fellow with alert eyes who could not be much more than an inch or two over five feet tall. He studied us intently as he bowed us in and then quickly shut and barred the door behind us. He seemed quite anxious.

"We have come from Lord Edmund's castle in the Bekka Valley to see the Bishop," I said in the bastardised French dialect some people are now calling English. And then Thomas repeated my words in Latin. *That is what I should have done in the first place.*

"I shall tell him you are here and ask if he will receive you," the man replied. "I am Yoram, the Bishop's scrivener; may I tell him who you are and why you are here?"

"I am William, the captain of the men who are left of the company of English archers who fought in the Bekka with Lord Edmund, and this is Father Thomas, our priest. We are here to collect our company's pay for helping to defend Lord Edmund's fief these past two years."

"I shall inform His Eminence of your arrival. Please wait here."

The Bishop's scrivener has a strange accent; I wonder how he came to be here?

Some time passed before the anxious little man returned. While he was gone we looked around the room. It was quite luxurious with a floor of stones instead of the mud floors one usually finds in a church.

The room was quite dark. The windows were covered with heavy wooden shutters and sealed shut with wooden bars; the light in the room, such as it was, came from cracks in the shutters and smaller windows high on the walls above the shuttered windows. There was a somewhat tattered tribal carpet on the floor.

The anxious little man returned and gave us a most courteous nod and bow.

"His Grace will see you now. Please follow me."

The Bishop's clerk led us into a narrow, dimly lit passage with stone walls and a low ceiling. He went first and then Thomas and then me. We had taken but a few steps when he turned back toward us and in a low voice issued a cryptic warning.

"Protect yourselves. The Bishop does not want to pay you. You are in mortal danger."

The little man nodded in silent agreement when I held up my hand. Thomas and I needed to take a moment to get ourselves ready.

He watched closely, and his eyes opened in surprise as we prepared ourselves. Then, when I gave a nod to let him know we were ready, he rewarded us with a tight smile and another nod—and began walking again with a determined look on his face.

A few seconds later we turned another corner and came to an open door. It opened into a large room with beamed ceilings more than six feet high. I knew the height because I could stand upright after I bent my head to get through the entrance door.

A portly older man in a bishop's robes was sitting behind a rough wooden table and there was a heavily bearded and rather formidable-looking guard with a sword in a wooden scabbard standing in front of the table. There was a closed chest on the table and a jumble of tools and chests in the corner covered by another old tribal rug and a broken chair.

The Bishop smiled to show us his yellow teeth and beckoned us in. We could see him clearly despite the dim light coming in from the small window openings near the ceiling of the room.

After a moment he stood and extended his hand over the table so we could kiss his ring. First Thomas and then I approached and half kneeled to kiss it. Then I stepped back and towards the guard to make room for Thomas so he could re-approach the table and stand next to me as the Bishop re-seated himself.

"What is it you want to see me about?" the Bishop asked in Latin.

He said it with a sincere smile and leaned forward expectantly.

"I am William, captain of the late Lord Edmund's English archers, and this is Father Thomas, our priest and confessor." *And my older brother, although I am not going to mention it at the moment.*

"How can that be? Another man was commanding the archers when I visited Lord Edmund earlier this year, and we made our arrangements."

"He is dead. He took an arrow in the arm and it turned purple and rotted until he died. Another took his place and now he is dead also. Now I am the captain of the company."

The Bishop crossed himself and mumbled a brief prayer under his breath. Then he looked at me expectantly and listened intently.

"We have come to get the money Lord Edmund entrusted to you to pay us. We looked for you before we left the valley, but Beaufort Castle was about to fall and you had already fled. So we followed you here; we have come to collect our company's pay."

"Of course. Of course. I have it right here in the chest.

"Aran," he said, nodding to the burly soldier standing next to me, "tells me there are eighteen of you. Is that correct?" *And how would he be knowing that?*

"Yes, Eminence, that is correct."

"Well then, four gold Constantinople coins for each man is seventy-two; and you shall have them here and now."

"No, Eminence, that is not correct."

I reached inside my tunic and pulled out the company's copy of the contract with Lord Edmund, and laid the parchment on the desk in front of him.

As I placed it on the table, I tapped it with my finger and casually stepped further to the side, and even closer to his swordsman, so Thomas could once again step into my place in front of the Bishop and nod his agreement confirming it was indeed in our contract.

"The contract calls for the company to be paid four gold bezant coins from Constantinople for each of eighty-seven men and six more coins to the company for each man that is killed or loses both of his eyes, arms, legs, or his ballocks.

"It sums to one thousand and twenty-six bezants in all—and I know you have them because I was present when Lord Edmund gave you more than enough coins for our contract and you agreed to pay them to us. So here we are. We want our bezants."

"Oh yes. So you are. So you are. Of course. Well, you shall certainly get what is due you. God wills it."

I sensed the swordsman stiffen as the Bishop said the words and opened the lid of the chest. The Bishop reached in with both hands and took a big handful of gold bezants in his left hand and placed them on the table.

He spread the gold coins out on the table and motioned Thomas forward to help him count as he reached back in to fetch another handful. I stepped further to the left and even closer to the guard so Thomas would have plenty of room to step forward to help the Bishop count.

Everything happened at once when Thomas leaned forward to start counting the coins. The Bishop reached again into his money chest as if to get another handful. This time he came out with a dagger—and lunged across the coins on the table to drive it into Thomas's chest with a grunt of satisfaction.

The swordsman next to me simultaneously began pulling his sword from its wooden scabbard. Killing us had all been prearranged. .....

**** End of the Sample Pages ****

The Archers and all the other stories in this medieval saga are available as eBooks. Search for *Martin Archer stories*. And, if you could please spare a moment, I would also very much appreciate it if you would give this story a review with as many stars as possible in order to encourage other readers.

And finally, I would also most sincerely appreciate your thoughts as to whether more stories should be written about the Company of Archers. I can be reached at martinarcherV@gmail.com. Cheers, and thank you once again. /s/Martin